THE MAKING OF IMAGINE

AZING

The solo collection Vol.1
The making of IMAGINE

Text: Azing Moltmaker
Editor: Azing Moltmaker
Publisher: Foundation Beatles Fan - Holland
Printers: Krips - Meppel - Holland
Translation into English: Roger Bruneel

FIRST EDITION
Numbers 1 up to 1500 are released in a numbered and signed edititon.

This book will be released in a numbered limited edition of 5000.

01224

FOUNDATION BEATLES FAN (Stichting Beatles Fan)
Bannewaard 24
1824 EC Alkmaar
The Netherlands

Contents:

The Making Of ... IMAGINE

PROLOGUE

I wish you a warm welcome to the first volume of another series of books. Having nearly completed the Album Collection and already launched the first two volumes of the Bootleg Collection, I now also embarking on the Solo Collection. This series of books will deal with the solo recordings of John, Paul, George and Ringo, in special "theme" books. I believe that there is no better album to start this serie than John's masterpiece IMAGINE. It is without any doubt the best documented solo LP ever made by anyone of The Beatles.

John and Yoko had decided to film the recording sessions. Several of these sessions have by now been released by Yoko on either video and/or DVD. She has also issued further IMAGINE outtakes on the ANTHOLOGY 4CD box.
Further session tapes were transmitted during the American radio programmes "The Lost Lennon Tapes".

After John's death a substantial amount of books have been published. Naturally, there were a couple of excellent ones amongst them, but the majority were made with the sole purpose of making a quick buck! As far as contents is concerned, they are usually very poor and badly documented. During my research for this book, I soon realized that it would not be an easy task to come up with a satisfactory and complete summary. Looking back now at the end product, I have proven myself wrong and am very satisfied with what has been achieved. The book comes with the usual structure, chapter one covers the recording sessions, who plays which instrument, which deviating versions there are and what has been released on bootlegs. It is unavoidable that somethings will be duplicated. Deviating versions and bootlegs and also reissues and compilations may include the same versions as they all originate from the same source. Notwithstanding this, I have elected to treat each song separately to achieve a complete picture. The second chapter is about the film, the record and the IMAGINE book which was released during the eighties. Chapter three concentrates on the DVD and the videos that are in circulationwith IMAGINE session outtakes.
Finally, the fourth chapter contains the discographies. First, the IMAGINE vinyl record, the singles from it, the compilation albums and the CDs that have been released over the years. Detailed information is given from the usual four countries, The United KIngdom, The United States Of America, Japan and The Netherlands. This is followed by various rare and unusual releases from all around the world. The chapter is concluded by the bootleg review, which in turn is divided in a vinyl and a CD section.

It is impossible to make a reference book like this on your own.
I would therefore like to thank the following Beatles collectors for their valued scans: Gerrit Braaksma,, Samuel Coomans, Ed Dieckmann, Hillebrand Peerdeman, Masanory Yokoono, Pete Nash, Frank Daniels and Frank Leenheer.
I also like to thank the German Beatles fanclub Beatlemania for their German Imagine' scans.

From our Foundation Beatles Fan team, I would like to thank Roger Bruneel for the translation, Ed and Mary van der Es for the corrections of the Dutch language publications, Maja van der Velde for her advice and naturally my sweet daughter Lisa for her support and understanding.

I dedicate this book to Maja! Due to her I started the Beatles Fan-club again. She also encouraged me to write my books about The Beatles. She thought me how to edit and to do the lay-out. She backed me when I could no longer cope and helped me unconditionally with all my Beatles projects.
Although we have now gone our separate ways, we will remain united eternally through our books about the Fab Four.

Thank you, Maja!!!

Azing Moltmaker,
Alkmaar, 5 November 2002.

2
IMAGINE
Words and Music by
JOHN LENNON
Moderately
C
Cmaj7
F
Im-ag - ine there's no heav - en
it's ea - sy if you try
no hell below us
A-bove us on - ly sky
Am/E
Im - ag - ine all the peo-
Copyright © 1971 NORTHERN SONGS LIMITED, 12 Bruton Street, Mayfair, London W1X7 AH, England
All rights for the United States of America, Canada, Mexico and the Philippines controlled by
MACLEN MUSIC, INC., c/o ATV MUSIC GROUP, 6255 Sunset Blvd., Hollywood, Calif. 90028
International Copyright Secured Made in U.S.A. All Rights Reserved

chapter 1

The IMAGINE LP Recording Sessions.

From all the solo LPs, IMAGINE seems to be the one that appeals most to the imagination of the fans. Now follows the story how the album was recorded, the background to the songs, the official and the not so official versions.

Due to the "Lost Lennon Tapes" and the video documentaries issued by Yoko, a great number of outtakes from the IMAGINE sessions have been brought into circulation. The songs will be discussed in the same order as they appear on the album.

'Imagine'
Acetate

The Sessions And The Studio

Most of the IMAGINE recording sessions took place at Tittenhurst Park, a magnificent white house, which John and Yoko purchased in 1969 for £150.000.

They moved into the 300 year old house in August of the same year. A lake was constructed on Yoko's request. John decided to build his own recording studio, which he called A.S.S., meaning Ascot Sound Studio. It contained the following equipment:

IMAGINE
3 track acetate

* 2 Struder B62 stereo tape recorders with 706 varispeed unit, serial numbers 2077 and 2078.
* 8 Dolby A361 noise reduction units.
* 2 EMT 140S stereo transistor ververberation plates with internally powered remote control, serial numbers 02802 and 02824.
* 1 GARRARD 401 record transcription deck with pick-up amplifier.
* 1 pair of UREI 1176LN compressors.
* 1 MARSHALL 5002 time modulator.
* QUAD 303 power amplifiers.
* 2 NEUMANN condenser microphones U87, serial numbers 8153 and 8154.
* 3 NEUMANN condenser microphones KM84i, serial numbers 4104, 4105 and 4095.
* 2 NEUMANN condenser microphones U47fet,

IMAGINE
Phil Spector Records
Testpressing

'Imagine'
First release
USA

serial numbers 3222 and 3224.
* 1 AKG condenser microphone C452.
* Direct injection boxes and headphone control boxes.
* 4 Acoustic separation screens (8' x 4') with window.
* BEYER microphone stands with boom arm.
* EVENTIDE FL201 instant Flanger.
* EVENTIDE 1745M digital delay.
* CROWN DC300 power amplifier.
* DOLBY A360 noise reduction units.

The IMAGINE recording sessions started in May 1971 at the A.S.S. Studio and John and Yoko allowed their 7-day long session to be filmed. They intended to release a film as well as a record. The majority of the film images would not be released until after John's untimely death.

'It's So Hard'
First release
USA

Several friends and known musicians were hired for the sessions such as:
Alan White and Jim Keltner on drums.
Klaus Voormann on bass.
Nicky Hopkins and Mike Pinder on keyboards.
Tom Evans, Andy Davis and Joey Molland on guitar.
King Curtis on saxophone.
Although Ringo was present during the session he did not do any drumming on the album.
The string section was played by the Flux Fiddlers, a group of musicians from the New York Philharmonic Orchestra. They were used during the overdubbing sessions during June and July 1971 at the Recordplant East Studio in New York.

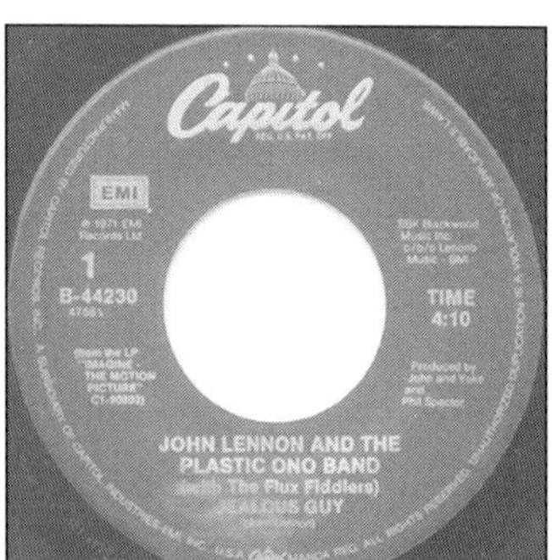

'Imagine'
1988 rerelease
USA

Not all the songs have film images, the ones we are aware of are: "Oh My Love", "Imagine", "How Do You Sleep?", "How", "Oh Yoko", "Give Me Some Truth" and "Jealous Guy".
Two 16 mm cameras were used for the filming, Nagra 1/4" recorders for the sound track and multitrack recorders for the album.

The first song to be filmed was "How Do You Sleep?". Rough working versions were shot. As we are not aware which numbers were filmed in full,, we can only use the videos IMAGINE, GIVE ME SOME TRUTH and THE MAKING OF IMAGINE (also on DVD) as evidence. It is also possible that all songs or some which I have not mentioned have also been filmed. A total of sixty hours of recording sessions have been shot and saved. The question is what will we ever be allowed to see? Only time will tell!!

'Imagine'
U.K.
First release

IMAGINE, The Sessions

Imagine

Written by John and Yoko.
Producers: John, Yoko and Phil Spector.
John: vocals and piano.
Klaus Voormann: bass.
Alan White: drums.
Flux Fiddlers: strike section.

'Imagine'
First release
The Netherlands

The title track was co-written by John and Yoko, although she is not mentioned on the record's credits. John would correct this during an interview in 1980. The inspiration originates from poems from the booklet GRAPEFRUIT, published by Yoko. The poems "Tunafish Sandwich Piece", "Painting To Be Constructed In Your Head", "Rubber Piece", "Cloud Piece" and "Pencil Lead Piece" all start with the word 'Imagine'. The American comedian Dick Gregory had given John a book with the title 'Positive Prayer'. It spurred John on to think positive. According to this book, everything is possible, providing you can imagine it and you believe in it yourself. It had a tremendous impact on John and he lived by it until his dying day. In an interview just before his death, John admitted that the song had actually been written by both himself and Yoko. At that time, he was thinking too much of himself to admit it. So, in this book, I am able to correct this minor misunderstanding by mentioning both names as the writers of the song.

'It's So Hard'
First release
The Netherlands

'Imagine'
First release
Germany

'Imagine'
First release
Germany

'Imagine'
First release
Germany

Deviating versions of "Imagine"

Apart from the version from the IMAGINE LP, there are also a number of deviating versions.

The IMAGINE LP has also been released in quadrophony. This is like a double stereo version, where the sound is divided over four tracks. You needed four speakers for this and each of them gives a different sound. For most of us, quadrophony was a luxury too far and like so many new inventions, it failed to make an impact. The quad LP was released in The United States with the catalogue number Apple QPAS 10004. It was pressed only once. It was also pressed in Australia, Germany, Great Britain and Japan. An 8-track also exists with sound variations. It is possible to listen to all four tracks separately. It was only released in the United States. In the U.K., EMI released the IMAGINE CD on 18 May 1987 with the catalogue number EMI CDS 7 46641 2. Here, the tapes had been adapted and the fade out of each song starts earlier than on the vinyl record. An alternative mix of "Imagine' can be found on the video/laser disc IMAGINE: JOHN LENNON by Warner Brothers 11819 and on the LP/CD version Parlophone PCSP 722/CD PCSP 722. Both were released in the U.K. on 10 October 1988. They had already been released in the U.S. on 4 October 1988 on vinyl and on CD with the catalogue numbers Capitol CI-90803/CDP 7 90803. Apart from the deviating mix of the existing song, this double LP/CD also contains a rehearsal version. On 2 November 1988 in the U.K. and one day later in the U.S., take 1 of "Imagine" was released on the 4CD set ANTHOLOGY, Capitol C2 8 30614 2. The recording can be found on CD1 ASCOT, track 9. A shortened version of take 1 is also on the compilation CD WONSAPONATIME, catalogue number Capitol 4 97639 2. This album was issued on 2 November 1998 on CD in the U.K. It also appeared as a one-off vinyl pressing on 18 January 1999, catalogue number Capitol 4 97639 1. The vinyl version was only released in Great Britain. The compilation CD was issued in the U.S. on 3 November 1998. A remastered IMAGINE CD appeared on the market on 14 February 2000.The original IMAGINE masters were remixed at Abbey Road by the same team that had remixed the YELLOW SUBMARINE SONG-TRACK. Besides the CD version with the catalogue number Parlophone 5 24858 2, a vinyl record also appeared in the U.K. on 27 March 2000 as Parlophone 5 24858 1.The remixed IMAGINE album was also released in the U.S. on 11 April 2000 as Capitol CDP 5 24858 2. Part of the sessions can also be found on the video and DVD GIVE ME SOME TRUTH, EMI 4 92348 9. It concerns a rehearsal and IMAGINE rendition behind the famous white grand piano.

'It's So Hard'
First release
Germany

"Imagine" on bootleg

As John and Yoko were used to record everything, Yoko was able to transmit a substantial amount of outtakes during the 'Lost Lennon Tapes' radio programmes. The Vigotone label has used these shows to put together an IMAGINE session outtakes compilation,, later completed by the Birthday Record label. Rather than having to collect and listen to the numerous 'Lost Lennon Tapes' vinyl LPs, fans only need to acquire the Vigotone or Birthday releases.

The first 5 volumes were first issued by Vigotone. They were then reissued by Birthday Records. Numbers 6 to 9 were released exclusively by Birthday Records. If you possess these 9 CDs, you have a complete picture about the IMAGINE outtakes that are in circulation up to now.

'Imagine'
Second rerelease
Germany

The following "Imagine" outtakes can be found on bootlegs:

'Imagine'
Second release
Germany

IMAGINE ALL THE OUTTAKES

Vigotone VT-188 - released in 1998.

1) Imagine - version 2, take 1.

'Imagine'
Rerelease
Germany

THE IMAGINE OUTTAKES
Birthday Records BR 015 - released in 1988.
1) Imagine - version 2, take 1.

IMAGINE ALL THE OUTTAKES Vol. 2
Vigotone VT-189 - released in 1998.

THE IMAGINE OUTTAKES Vol. 2
Birthday Records BR 016 - released in 1998.
1) Imagine - take 1.
2) Imagine - take 2.
3) Imagine - take 3.
4) Imagine - alternative vocals.
18) Imagine - rehearsal.

'Imagine'
Rerelease
Germany

MORE SESSIONS TAPES
Vigotone 185/86 - released in 1999.

THE IMAGINE OUTTAKES Vol. 4
Birthday Records BR 070 - released in 2000.
17) Imagine - alternate take.

Live renditions of "Imagine":

The first time John performed "Imagine" live was during the Attica State Benefit concert at the Apollo Theatre in New York on 17 December 1971. It was John and Yoko's second concert in the U.S. The concert was given for the family and acquaintences of inmates from Attica State prison. The show where John performs "Imagine" and "Attica State" was released in stereo on Capitol C2 8 30614 2, CD2 NEW YORK CITY, tracks 2 and 3 on 2 November 1998 in the U.K. and one day later in the U.S. The concert, where Yoko also performs "Sisters O Sisters", was filmed with a 16mm camera and is waiting to be released on video and DVD.

'Imagine' 7 inch
1981 rerelease
Germany

John and Yoko gave two live shows at Madison Square Gardens in New York on 30 August 1972. These were charity events for the benefit of the children from Willowbrook House in New York.

The first concert was sold out that fast that a second one had to be arranged. John and Yoko had drawn the public's attention to this second concert,,amongst others, by the use of radio spots. Both concerts were recorded under the supervision of Phil Spector. The recordings were shelved until 1987. The "Imagine" version originates from the afternoon show. A compilation was made from the two concerts and put on record and CD as well as on video and laserdisc.
The American television station ABC transmitted the evening concert on 14 December 1972. The same concert was also transmitted live via the radio netwerk KING BISCUIT. These recordings have been released on bootleg, I will come back to this later.
The total proceeds for the concert were $1,5 million.
There is a noticeable difference between the video version and the one on the LP, CD and the laserdisc where the music plays at the right speed. On the video, the music sounds slower. The live rendition of "Imagine" has been released officially on the LP/CD set LIVE IN NEW YORK CITY.
Parlophone PCS 7301 - vinyl - U.K. - released on 24 February 1986.
Parlophone CDP 7 46196 2 - CD - U.K. - released on 28 April 1986.
Capitol SV-12451 - vinyl - U.S.A. - released on 27 January 1986.
Capitol CDP 7 46196 2 - CD - U.S.A. - released on 26 May 1986. It has also been issued on laserdisc Pioneer Artist PA-86-162 and on Video VHS MVP 991101 2 and Betamax MXP991101 4.

'Imagine' 12 inch
1981 release
Germany

'Imagine' 12 inch
1981 release
Germany

'Imagine'
Second 12 inch release
Germany

THE IMAGINE OUTTAKES VOL. 6
Birthday Records BR 087 - released in 2001.
1) Imagine - slower version.
This originates from the IMAGINE film.

THE IMAGINE OUTTAKES VOL. 7
Birthday Records BR 088 - released in 2001.
1) Imagine - quad miz.
2) Channel stereo - from the quadrophonic IMAGINE LP/8 track.

'Imagine'
Second 12 inch release
Germany

'Imagine'
3rd release -Dutch sleeve
Germany

'Imagine'
3rd release - German sleeve
Germany

THE IMAGINE OUTTAKES VOL. 8
Birthday Records BR 089 - released in 2001.
2) Imagine - piano rehearsal.
3) Imagine - John discussing with Phil Spector.
4) Imagine - different mix, used for the making of Imagine film, 2 different parts.
These recordings originate from the DVD GIVE ME SOME TRUTH.

THE IMAGINE OUTTAKES VOL. 9
Birthday Records BR 090 - released in 2001.
1) Imagine - centre mix.
2) Imagine - front channels.
3) Imagine - rear channels.
These are the so-called 5.1 Surround mixes, where the channels have been separated and the tracks can be listened to separately. They also originate from the GIVE ME SOME TRUTH DVD.

Live renditions of "Imagine" on bootlegs:

John has performed the song several times live. Luckily, these versions have been saved and can be found on the following bootlegs:

Hotel Syracuse, New York, U.S.A.
Recorded on 9 October 1971.
John celebrated his 31st birthday on 9 October 1971 at the Syracuse Hotel in New York with a great number of friends such as Ringo and Maureen Starr, Phil Spector, Klaus Voormann, Jim Keltner and Allen Ginsberg. This venue was chosen because Yoko's exhibition 'This Is Not Here' took place at the same hotel.
The recordings from the party can be found on two different bootlegs. The first one is LETS HAVE A PARTY with a playing time of only 49 minutes. The second CD, with a longer playing time, is titled JOHN LENNON'S 31ST BIRTHDAY PARTY, catalogue number Rockin' Records JLBP-01. The "Imagine' song, amongst others, was also played at this party and just like most other events in John and Yoko's lives, it was filmed. These images can be seen in the

video/DVD documentary GIVE ME SOME TRUTH.

ATTICA STATE BENEFIT

Apollo Theatre, New York, U.S.A.

Recorded on 17 December 1971.

This is the first time that John performed the song live in front of the public. The recordings first appeared in 1982. The Bag One Label,, that would also issue the LOST LENNON SHOWS, were the first to release the record on the YING YANG LP, catalogue number Bag 5071. The mix that we can hear on this record is the same as on the bootleg CDs ACOUSTIC MASTER PIECE on Birthday Records BR 012, THE IMAGINE OUTTAKES VOL. 6 on Birthday Records BR 087 and UNPLUGGED (JL901). The difference in recording is that all the above bootlegs come with a mono mix where as the officially released version on the ANTHOLOGY set is a stereo mix.

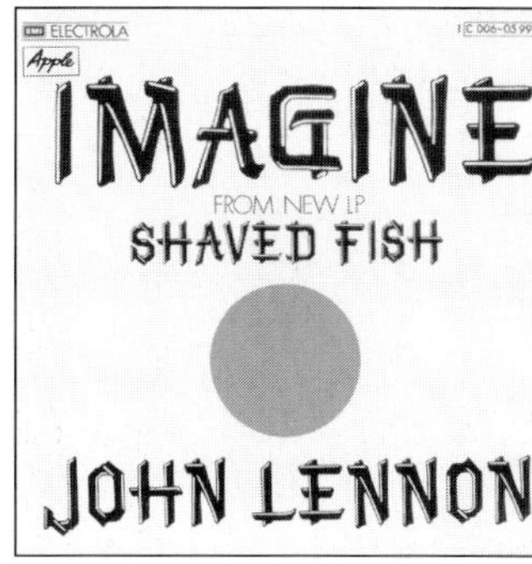

'Imagine'
4rd release
Germany

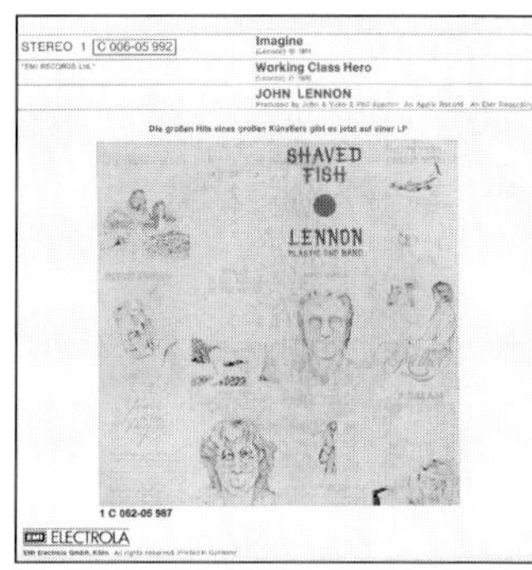

'Imagine'
4rd release
Germany

THE MIKE DOUGLAS SHOW

WBC Studios, Philadelphia, U.S.A.

Recorded on 27 January 1972.

Broadcas on 17 February 1972.

John and Yoko were presenting the Mike Douglas Shows from 14 to 18 February 1972, being the transmission dates. John performed "Imagine" during the fourth show. The shows were recorded over 5 days at the Westinghouse Broadcasting Corporations Studios in Philadelphia. The recording dates were 14, 18, 20, 27 and 28 January 1972. The five shows were broadcast again in full by the music television channel VH-1 in December 1996. A 5 part video set was also released in the U.S. by Rhino. The recordings could be found for the first time during the seventies on the bootleg LP TELECAST (wec 3711). It was reissued later on in the seventies, with a better sound quality and a well designed colour LP cover, with the same title and with the catalogue number JL517. On CD, the shows appeared on the bootleg CD TELECAST on Contra Band 3711.

The Birthday Record label issued the show on their CD IMAGINE OUTTAKES VOL. 6 on BR 087.

'Imagine'
4rd release
Germany

'Imagine'
1988 release
Germany

'Imagine'
1988 release
Germany

'Imagine'
1988 release
Germany

ONE TO ONE BENEFIT
Madison Square Gardens, New York, U.S.A.
Recorded on 30 August 1972 - Matinee show.
As well as the introduction to the evening concert, the live version of this concert can be found on the record LIVE IN NEW YORK.
A recording in front of the public can also be found on the bootlegs ONE TO ONE CONCERTS by Zeus Z 904001 and THE IMAGINE OUTTAKES VOL. 6 by Birthday Records BR 087.

ONE TO ONE BENEFIT
Madison Square Gardens, New York, U.S.A.
Recorded on 30 August 1972 - Evening show.
The evening show has also been released on bootleg several times. ABC television's recordings can, amongst others, be found on the vinyl bootleg ONE TO ONE CONCERT AND MORE by Wizardo WRMB 301 and the King Biscuit mix is on the CDs JOHN, PAUL, GEORGE AND RINGO on YD-Orange 020 and IMAGINE OUTTAKES VOL. 6 by Birthday Records BR 087. There is also a live concert in front of the public on ONE TO ONE CONCERTS by Zeus Z 904003.
The recordings have been reissued several times on vinyl.

JERRY LEWIS LABOR DAY TELETHON
Americana Hotel, New York, U.S.A.
Recorded and transmitted live on 6 September 1972.
During this show, John performed the songs "Imagine", "Now And Never" and "Give Peace A Chance". The recordings can be found on the bootleg CDs MISCELLANEOUS TRACKS on YD-Orange 018 and IMAGINE OUTTAKES on Birthday BR 087.

SALUTE TO SIR LEW GRADE
ABC TV, U.S.A.
Recorded on 18 April 1975 and broadcast on 13 June 1975. John's last public appearance; he performed three songs, "Stand By Me", "Slippin' And

Slidin'" and "Imagine".
A remixed version of the "Imagine" song can be found on the JOHN LENNON COLLECTION video and the CD single & CD-r "Imagine" which was released in 1999. The song "Slippin' And Slidin'" was not broadcast during the show, although there is a recording of the complete show that has been issued on CD. These can be found on the CDs WARSHIP THE LORD YOUR GOD AND SERVE HIM ONLY by Master Of Orange MOO-10006 and ROCK AND ROLL SESSIONS VOL. 3 by Birthday BR 074. The recording of the television broadcast has been reissued several times over the years. The best sound quality can be found on MISCELLANEOUS TRACKS on YD-Orange 018 and IMAGINE OUTTAKES VOL. 6 by Birthday BR 089.

'Imagine'
First release
France

"Imagine" sung by Paul.

KING DOCK ARENA, LIVERPOOL.
Recorded on 28 June 1990.
Prior to Paul's concert with his band in Liverpool, he played "Imagine" during the rehearsals. It had been the intention to play the song in a Lennon-medley.
Although he did make a medley with "Help!", "Strawberry Fields Forever" and "Give Peace A Chance", he did not perform "Imagine" in front of the public. Although both the soundcheck and the concert have been filmed, this "Imagine" version is still not in circulation yet. Considering the success of this Lennon medley, Paul has carried on playing it a number of times 'live' although he has still not performed "Imagine" in front of the public.
So, we still have to wait for the bootleg release of the Liverpool Soundcheck.

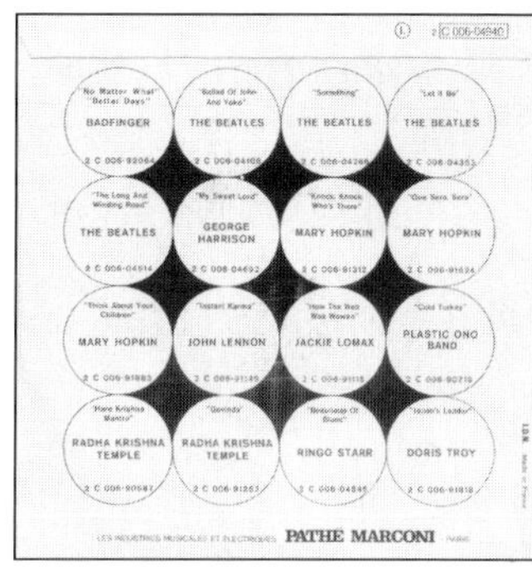

'Imagine'
First release
France

'Imagine'
First release
France

Crippled Inside

'It's So Hard'
First release
France

Written by John.
Producers: John, Yoko and Phil Spector.
John: vocals and electric guitar.
Klaus Voormann - upright bass.
Steve Brendell - upright bass.
George Harrison: dobro.
Nicky Hopkins: piano.
Ted Turner: acoustic guitar.
Rod Linton: acoustic guitar.
John Tout: acoustic guitar.

Just like the song "How Do You Sleep?" (see later in this chapter), this is also an attack on Paul. In the song John accuses Paul of being a living lie. As the attack on Paul is less obvious then in "How Do You Sleep?", the fans did not notice it at first. In interviews John did not discuss it either. On this song, George plays a dobro, which is a special acoustic guitar with a metal sound chamber, named after their inventors, the Dopera brothers. These are two guitar makers coming from Chechoslovakia, who immigrated to the U.S.A. For the music John had been inspired by "Black Dog Blues" which had been released in 1920 by Blind Blake. That John was aware of this record can already be heard during the Get Back Sessions of January 1969. The recording of this track as a Beatles version can be found on the bootleg CDs JAMMING WITH HEATHER (BECD 001), THE GET BACK JOURNALS IV Disc Seven-Eight by Birthday BR 057/58 and GET BACK CAMERA B-ROLLS VOL. 11 by Unicorn UC-122/13.

'Imagine'
First release
Norway

'Imagine'
First release
Denmark

Deviating versions of "Crippled Inside"

Apart from the version on the IMAGINE LP, there are also a number of deviating versions.
There is also a quadrophonic version of the IMAGINE LP as well as 8-track, where the tracks can be played separately; details of both can be found in the deviating versions of "Imagine".
EMI released the IMAGINE CD on 18 May 1987 in the U.K., catalogue number EMI CDS 7 46641 2.

On this CD, the fade out of all the tracks start earlier than on the vinyl LP. The remastered IMAGINE CD appeared on 14 February 2000, mixed at Abbey Road from the original IMAGINE masters. There is also a vinyl version which was pressed in the U.K. only. The CD was also released in the U.S. on 11 April 2000. Part of this session can also be heard on the video and DVD GIVE ME SOME TRUTH on EMI 4 92348 9. For the film that was played at the Cannes Film Festival, the song got a different mix. This one has never been released.

'My Love'/'Give Me Some Truth'
Japan

"Crippled Inside" on bootleg

The song has never been performed live by John and even from the recording sessions, there is very little in circulation. There is a deviating mix from the released take 17 on the CDs IMAGINE ALL THE OUTTAKES by Vigotone VT-188 and THE IMAGINE OUTTAKES VOL. 1 by Birthday BR 015.

The majority of take 2 can be heard on the CDs IMAGINE ALL THE OUTTAKES by Vigotone VT-189 and THE IMAGINE OUTTAKES VOL. 2 by Birthday BR 016. The song's intro is missing whilst it was in show 88-33/5 of the Lost Lennon Tapes presented. In case you are confused about the show numbers, 88 is the year, 33 is the number of the show and 5 is the number of the track. The shows were pressed on vinyl LPs and thus sent to the American radio stations. It must be possible to compose a complete number from these two parts. It will only be a question of time before the 'Lost Lennon Tape' version and the bootleg version are fused. The version that can be seen in the IMAGINE film is on the CD IMAGINE OUTTAKES VOL. 6 by Birthday BR 087. There is a quadrophonic mix on IMAGINE OUTTAKES VOL. 7 by Birthday BR 088. The recordings from the GIVE ME SOME TRUTH DVD can be found on IMAGINE OUTTAKES VOL. 8 by Birthday BR 089; the house party recordings from early 1970 are also on this CD. Finally, the 5.1 Surround mixes are on IMAGINE OUTTAKES VOL. 9 by Birthday BR 090.

'Imagine'
2000 single-cd rerelease

'Imagine'
Still sealed 12 inch rerelease
Germany

'Jealous Guy'
Japan

'Jealous Guy'
Spain

'Jealous Guy'
Brazil

Jealous Guy

Written by John.
Producers: John, Yoko and Phil Spector.
John: vocals, flute and guitar.
Klaus Voormann: bass.
Jim Keltner: drums.
John Barham: harmonium.
Alan White: good vibes.

This song goes back to 1968, that is when John wrote it in Rishikes in India, although it still had the title "Child Of Nature". It first had the work title "On The Road To Marakesh". During the Esher Sessions, that took place during the third week of may 1968, the song "Child Of Nature" had already been recorded in an acoustic version at George's house. This version can be found on the bootleg CDs ACOUSTIC MASTERPIECES by Birthday BR 029 and FROM KIMFAUNS TO CHAOS by Vigotone VT-183/184. Although both bootlegs use the Esher tapes, there are some differences between them. The Birthday release, which was also in circulation as UNPLUGGED, contains the recordings from John's tape, whilst the Vigotone release uses George's tape. As far as sound quality is concerned both CDs are virtually identical although the Vigotone version has a longer playing time. John has also played and recorded the song with The Beatles during the Get Back Sessions. Even when John was already working on the IMAGINE LP, he recorded "Child Of Nature" once more in a medley. I will list all the versions in the bootleg review.

John dropped his original lyrics and rewrote the song during the IMAGINE sessions. The lyrics are about John looking at himself in the mirror, the jealous guy being himself. Towards Yoko, he behaved extremely possessive. He demanded that she made a list of all the men she had been with before they met.

He was troubled that he could not understand her when she spoke Japanese with her family and felt excluded. With "Jealous Guy", John tried to relate to the bad side of his character. The song received

excellent arrangements from Phil Spector.
Drummer Alan White was present during the session but did not drum on the recording, although he has been credited on the inner cover for his 'good vibes'.
The song was recorded on 24 May 1972 in John's studio.

'Jealous Guy'
Single-CD
Netherlands

Deviating versions of "Jealous Guy"

Apart from the version that can be found on the IMAGINE LP, there are also a number of that deviate. The LP was also released in quadrophony, details of this can be found in the deviating versions of "Imagine". The LP has also been released as an 8-track, where the four tracks can be listened to separately. On the CD release of the IMAGINE LP, the fade out of all the songs starts earlier than on the vinyl LP. An alternative mix of "Jealous Guy" can be found on the video/laserdisc IMAGINE: JOHN LENNON by Warner Brother 11819 and the LP/CD versions released in 1988 in both the U.K. and the U.S.A. This version comes with deviating vocals, the string section has been erased and the playing time has been reduced to 2.40 minutes. One can also hear some studio talk and whistling by John. For the release of the LENNON VIDEO COLLECTION in the U.K. on 5 October 1992 on PMI MVNC 4910343, the song got a different mix and some studio sounds were added. Another deviating mix of "Jealous Guy" was released in 1988 on the 4CD set ANTHOLOGY in both the U.S.A. and the U.K. The mix can be found on CD1 ASCOT, track 13. A remastered version of the IMAGINE LP appeared on CD in the U.K. and the U.S.A in 2000. A one-off vinyl pressing also appeared in the U.K. only. Part of the session can also be heard on the video and DVD GIVE ME SOME TRUTH. The song got a further deviating mix for the film shown at the Cannes Film Festival. This version has never been released.
The recording session of "Jealous Guy" can be admired in the documentary.

'Jealous Guy'
Single-CD
The Netherlands

'Imagine'
Music postcard
Polland

"Child Of Nature" on bootleg

'Jealous Guy'
France

"Jealous Guy" in its early version of "Child Of Nature" already in 1968 issued. John recorded it several times with The Beatles. Up to date, The Beatles version has not been released. I have already mentioned the Esher version and the Get Back Sessions before. I will now elaborate on both one at a time.

'Jealous Guy'
France

Jealous Guy'
France

During their stay in India, The Beatles had already written a great deal of songs and the oldest known version of the song was recorded during the third week of May 1968. The Beatles met at George's house to record all the songs they had written there in a long acoustic session. George had named his house KIMFAUNS and it was located in ESHER. Both names can be found back on several bootlegs. They refer to the Esher sessions and the Kinfauns demos. Both refer to the same recordings. Finally, each one of The Beatles took a copy of the tape home with him. Yoko has played a great part of John's tape during the "Lost Lennon Tapes" shows. The 'John' tape would be reissued several times over the years. It first appeared on the ninth bootleg of the 'Lost Lennon Tapes'. The LP was issued with a beautiful psychedelic album cover and was called NUMBER NINE, with Volume 9 crossed off. The LP's catalogue number is BAG 5081 and "Child Of Nature" is the first track of side B. It was then reissued by Yellow Dog in 1991with the title UNSURPASSED DEMOS, YD 008. The sound quality was only average. The recordings were issued with better sound quality on the bootleg CD UNPLUGGED (TH 001 and distributed on the 3CD set OFF WHITE (PPCD 1136/1138). All these bootlegs had one thing in common, played at the wrong speed on some of the songs. The recordings were reissued, for the first time in a cleaned up version, by Birthday Records BR 029 on the CD ACOUSTIC MASTERPIECES. This CD-r was then reissued by other bootleggers on silver CDs. This is the best sound quality in circula-

tion of the 'John' tape.
The Vigotone label came up with a different tape. On their double CD FROM KINFAUNS TO CHAOS VT-183/184 they released the tape that had belonged to George. When one listens to the tapes, small differences can be heard. George's tape sounds cleared and plays a little bit longer.

'Jealous Guy'
TheNetherlands

John did not record the song with The Beatles during the WHITE ALBUM recording sessions.
During the Get Back Sessions, he had a couple more goes at it. He played it with The Beatles on 2 and 24 January 1969. The 2 January 1969 version can be found on the bootlegs THE FIRST RECORDED HOUR OF THE LET IT BE SESSIONS by Yellow Dog YDB 104 and GET BACK JOURNALS 3 by Birthday. The 24 January 1969 version is on THE GET BACK JOURNALS 1 by Vigotone VT-107, CD7, track 21. It is not known whether John played the song at any other time during the Get Back Sessions. Notwithstanding the fact that John played the song a number of times with The Beatles, it has never been released as a Beatles version.

'Jealous Guy'
The Netherlands

Even during the JOHN LENNON AND THE PLASTIC ONO BAND sessions, the song remained untouched. But, during the IMAGINE sessions John came back to it. He only recorded "Child Of Nature" once with its original lyrics. It was recorded in a medley with "How?" and "Oh Yoko". This version can be found on the bootleg CDs IMAGINE... ALL THE OUTTAKES by Vigotone VT 190 and THE IMAGINE OUTTAKES VOL. 1 by Birthday BR 017.
After this, John altered the lyrics to "Jealous Guy" and included it on the IMAGINE LP.

'Imagine'
Promo only
Japan

"Jealous Guy" on bootlegs

Various outtakes of the song have been released on bootleg. The alternate take was broadcast for the first time during the 'Lost Lennon Shows' and this version was in the programme 88-24/1. This same alternate version has always been used. First there was the "Lost Lennon' version and then it came in a diffe-

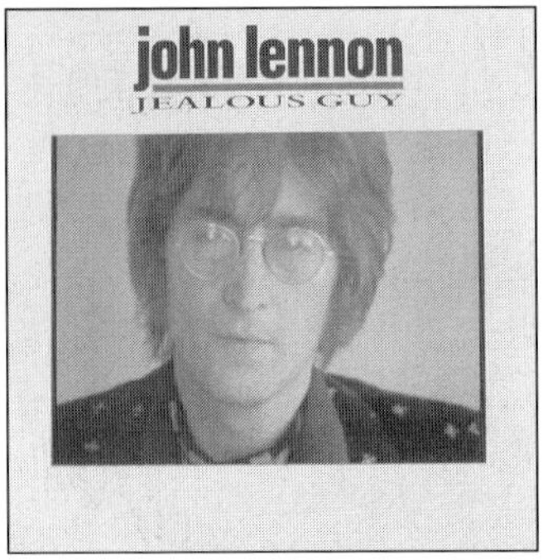

'Jealous Guy'
12 ich release
UK

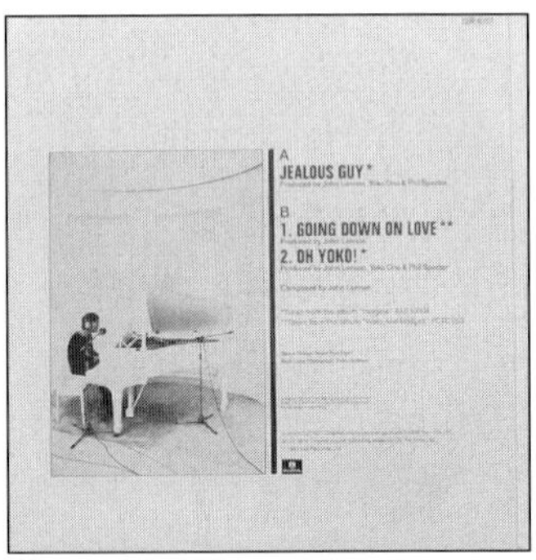

'Jealous Guy'
12 inch release
UK

'Jealous Guy'
12 inch release
UK

rent mix on the CD IMAGINE.... ALL THE OUTTAKES by Vigotone VT-188 and THE IMAGINE OUTTAKES VOL. 1 by Birthday BR 015.
Finally, another deviating version appeared, this time officially on the ANTHOLOGY set. It is unusual that the count down can only be heard on the 'Lost Lennon' shows version. The Vigotone/Birthday mix is dryer and mixed more towards the front. On the officially released version, the harmonium is clearer and there is a longer fade out. Take 2 can be heard on the CD IMAGINE ... ALL THE OUTTAKES by Vigotone VT-189 and THE IMAGINE OUTTAKES VOL. 1 by Birthday BR 016. This version can also be heard on the DVD version of GIVE ME SOME TRUTH. Apart from take 2, the above mentioned CDs also feature take 7 and vocal take 20.
The IMAGINE film version is on the CD IMAGINE OUTTAKES VOL. 6 by Birthday BR 087. There is a quadrophonic mix on IMAGINE OUTTAKES VOL. 7 by Birthday BR 088. The DVD version of GIVE ME SOME TRUTH is on IMAGINE OUTTAKES VOL. 8 by Birthday BR 089. The Esher and Get Back versions can also be heard on this CD. Finally, the 5.1 Surround mixes are on IMAGINE OUTTAKES VOL. 9 by Birthday BR 090.

It's So Hard

Written by John.
Producers: John, Yoko and Phil Spector.
John: vocals and guitar.
Klaus Voormann: bass.
Jim Gordon: drums.
King Curtis: saxophone.

This song's work title was "Going Down". It was the first song to be recorded in John's studio. He used this one to test his studio equipment. The song is an extension from the LP JOHN LENNON AND THE PLASTIC ONO BAND. The lyrics carry on where the LP ended. This happens with more songs which were recorded during the IMAGINE sessions.
For this John was assisted by the legendary saxopho-

ne player King Curtis. John was a great admirer of this musician. The overdubbing sessions took place on 4 July 1971 at the Record Plant Studio in New York. King Curtis was not able to witness the release of the IMAGINE LP. On 13 August 1971, only six weeks after this session, the 37 year old King Curtis was stabbed outside his apartment in New York by Juan Montanez from Puerto Rico. Originally, part of John's sessions could be seen at Allen Kleins appartment in New York in the documentary "Imagine The Motion Picture". These 40 seconds were cut from the film and even for the video/DVD GIVE ME SOME TRUTH, these images were no longer used. The song was used for the single's B-side in The United States.

'Oh Yoko!'
12 inch release
UK

Deviating versions of "It's So Hard"

Apart from the version on the IMAGINE LP, there are also a number of deviating ones.
The IMAGINE LP was also released in quadrophony. There exist also an 8-track version where the four tracks can be listened to separately. On the CD version which was released in 1987, the fade out of all the songs starts earlier than on the vinyl LP.
The song received another mix for the DVD GIMME SOME TRUTH.

'Jealous Guy'
USA

Live renditions of "It's So Hard"

John did play the song live during the ONE TO ONE Concerts in New York on 30 August 1972. The afternoon show has been officially released in 1986 in both the U.K. and the U.S.A, on CD and as a one-off on vinyl in the U.K. only. It was released on video and laserdisc in the U.S. on 24 January 1986 on Pioneer Artist PA-86-196. In the U.K. it was also released on video on VHS (MVP99 1101 2) and Betamax (MXP 99 1101 4. The evening concert was released by Yoko on the 4CD set ANTHOLOGY in 1998 in both the U.K. and the U.S.A.
The live version can be found on CD2 NEW YORK CITY, track 8.

'Jealous Guy'
USA

IMAGINE
EP
Mexico

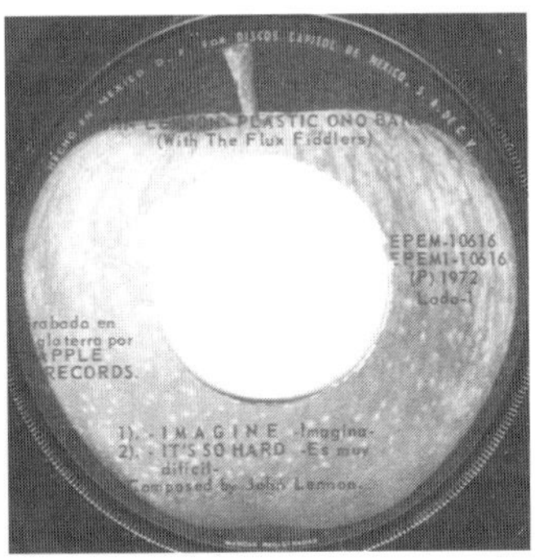

IMAGINE
EP
Mexico

IMAGINE
EP
Mexico

"It's So Hard" on bootleg

Take 2 of the recording session can be found on the bootleg CDs IMAGINE ... ALL THE OUTTAKES by Vigotone VT-188 and THE IMAGINE OUTTAKES VOL. 1 by Birthday BR 015. This originates from the sessions at the A.S.S studios. It is the same take that was actually used for the IMAGINE LP, but without the saxophone overdubs. The recordings at the A.S.S. studios complete, John, Yoko and Phil Spector went to the Record Plant Studios in New York on 4 July 1971 to do the overdubs with King Curtis and the mixing. John has recorded the sessions on tape and saved with pride. The tape was then transmitted partially during the 'Lost Lennon Tapes'. This happened in show 90-06/3 and 92-023 and 4. Whilst Lennon and Spector were busy with the overdubs of "Jealous Guy", King Curtis entered the studio. He just left the Newport Jazz Festival and was tired. But work takes very priority and they went straight at it. The following recordings from this session have been released on bootlegs:

1) John starts tape.
2) King Curtis arrives.
3) Intro Playback.
4) John demonstrates on acoustic.
5) King Curtis riffs.
6) First pass and more riffing.
7) Second Pass.
8) King Curtis asks John a question.
9) Third Pass.
10) John gives King Curtis feedback.
11) Another pass at the intro.
12) Another pass at the intro 2.
13) Last pass.

The sessions can be found on the following bootlegs CDs: IMAGINE ... MORE SESSIONS TAPES by Vigotone VT-185/186 and THE IMAGINE OUTTAKES VOL. 5 by Birthday BR 071. The version from the IMAGINE film can be found on the CD IMAGINE OUTTAKE VOL. 6 by Birthday BR 087.

A quadrophonic mix is on the IMAGINE OUTTAKES VOL. 7 by Birthday BR 088.
The recording from the DVD GIVE ME SOME TRUTH can be found on THE IMAGINE OUTTAKES VOL. 8 by Birthday BR 089. Finally, the 5.1 Surround mixes of the song are on IMAGINE OUTTAKES VOL. 9 by Birthday BR 090.

'Imagine'
1981 rerelease
The Netherlands

Live renditions of "It's So Hard" on bootleg

Just like with the song "Imagine", John has performed "It's So Hard" several times. These recordings have fortunately been saved. Some have been issued officially and others have remained in Yoko's archivesor at the radio stations. Due to the bootlegs, we can also hear these versions.

'Imagine'
1981 rerelease
The Netherlands

The Mike Douglas Show
WBC Studios, Philadelphia, U.S.A.
Recorded on 14 January 1972.
Broadcast on 14 February 1972.
John and Yoko were presenting the show between 14 and 18 February 1972. In the first of five shows which was recorded on 14 January 1972 and transmitted on 14 February 1972, John performed "It's So Hard". The recordings were available for the first time on the bootleg LP TELECAST (Wec 3711) was reissued in the seventies, with a better sound quality, with the same title and the catalogue number JL517. On CD it appeared as TELECAST by Contra Band 3711 and THE IMAGINE OUTTAKES VOL. 6 by Birthday BR 087.

'It's So Hard'
1981 rerelease
The Netherlands

ONE TO ONE REHEARSALS
Butterfly Studios, New York, U.S.A.
Recorded on 18 August 1972.
Rehearsals took place prior to John and his Plastic Ono Band 's appearance at Madison Square Gardens. Not less than 20 songs were rehearsed and one of them was "It's So Hard". The rehearsals appeared for the first time during the seventies as a 3LP set ONE AND ONE AND ONE ARE THREE by Benefit

'Imagine'
Italy

'It's So Hard'
Italy

'Imagine'
Italy

Records 001/3. "It's So Hard" can be found on LP1, Side A. The LPs have been released by the same people who later released it on CD with the title ONE TO ONE REHEARSALS VOL. 1 by Orange Sixteen.Further rehearsals for these concerts took place on 21 and 22 August 1972, but this time the song "It's So Hard" was not played.

ONE TO ONE BENEFIT
Madison Square Gardens, New York, U.S.A.
Recorded on 30 August 1972 - Afternoon show.
This version of "It's So Hard" has also been released officially on the LP/CD LIVE IN NEW YORK CITY. There are also live recordings on the bootlegs ONE TO ONE CONCERTS by Zeus Z 904001 and IMAGINE OUTTAKES VOL. 6 by Birthday BR 087.

ONE TO ONE BENEFIT
Madison Square Gardens, New York, U.S.A.
Recorded on 30 August 1972 - evening concert.
This show has also been released on bootleg several times.The ABC television version is, amongst others, on the vinyl bootleg ONE TO ONE CONCERT AND MORE by Wizardo WRMB 301. A live recording can also be found on ONE TO ONE CONCERTS by Zeus Z 904003 and IMAGINE OUTTAKES VOL. 6 by Birthday BR 087. This concert has been reissued many times on vinyl records. The recording has also been released officially on the ANTHOLOGY CD-set.

I Don't Want To Be A Soldier (Mama, I Don't Wanna Die)

Written by John.
John: vocals and guitar.
Klaus Voormann: bass.
Jim Keltner: drums.
George Harrison: slide guitar.
Nicky Hopkins: piano.
Joe Molland: acoustic guitar.
Tom Evans: acoustic guitar.
Mike Pinder: tambourine.
Steve Brendell: maracas.
King Curtis: saxophone.
Producers: John, Yoko and Phil Spector.

According to John this song was nothing more than a jamming session. John let us hear his disgust towards violence. Following "Give Peace A Chance" this was his next anti-war song. Amongst the many musicians who assisted with this song were Joe Molland and Tom Evans. Both members of the Apple band Badfinger would finally commit suicide by hanging themselves. John, like all other three Beatles, never has done any army service. Compulsory service had been abolished in the late fifties.

'It's So Hard'
Italy

'Jealous Guy'
Thailand

Deviating versions of "I Don't Want To Be A Soldier":

Apart from the version on the IMAGINE LP, there are also a number of deviating ones.
The IMAGINE LP was also released in quadrophony and an extra saxophone has been added. An 8-track also exists and all four tracks can be listened to separately. On the CD that was released in 1987, the fade out of all the songs starts earlier than on the vinyl LP.
The recording of take 2 has been released by Yoko Ono on the 4CD set ANTHOLOGY. This version can be found on CD1, ASCOT, track 18.
The song received another mix for the DVD GIVE ME SOME TRUTH.

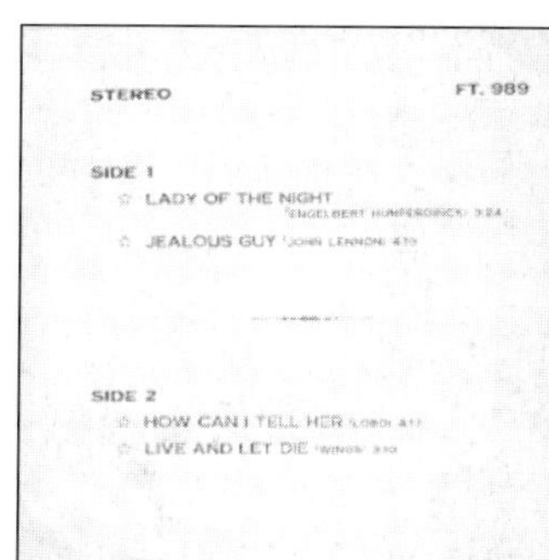

'Jealous Guy'
Thailand

'Jealous Guy'
1988 release
UK

'Jealous Guy'
1988 release
UK

'Imagine'
1988 release
UK

"I Don't Want To Be A Soldier" on bootleg

Three versions from the A.S.S. sessions have been issued on bootlegs. Take 2 can be found on the CDs IMAGINE ... ALL THE OUTTAKES by Vigotone VT-188 and THE IMAGINE OUTTAKES VOL. 1 by Birthday BR 015. Take 1 and an alternate mix can be found on the CDs IMAGINE ... ALL THE OUTTAKES by Vigotone VT-189 and THE IMAGINE OUTTAKES VOL. 2 by Birthday BR 016. The saxophone overdubbing session from 4 July 1971 can be heard, partially, on the CDs IMAGINE... ALL THE OUTTAKES by Vigotone VT-189 and THE IMAGINE OUTTAKES VOL. 3 by Birthday BR 017. The overdubbing session with King Curtis is more complete on the CDs IMAGINE MORE SESSIONS by Vigotone VT-185/186 and THE IMAGINE OUTTAKES VOL. 5 by Birthday BR 071. The saxophone overdubbing has been constructed as follows:

14) John discusses the 1966 tour.
15) First playback.
16) Playback continued, the first 'Hit It'.
17) Playback continued, the second 'Hit It'.
18) John and King Curtis talk.
19) First pass.
20) John instructs King Curtis.
21) Second pass.
22) Third pass.
23) Last pass.

John encourages King Curtis to play as wild as possible. Thirty minutes of this session have been saved, and than John's tape cut off. Parts of the session were first transmitted in the shows 90-06 and 92-02 of the 'Lost Lennon Tapes'. The version from the IMAGINE film is on the CD THE IMAGINE OUTTAKES VOL. 6 by Birthday BR 087. There is a quadrophonic mix on THE IMAGINE OUTTAKES VOL. 7 by Birthday BR 088. The version from the DVD GIVE ME SOME TRUTH is on THE IMAGINE OUTTAKES VOL. 8 by Birthday BR 089.Finally, the 5.1 Surround mixes can be found on THE IMAGINE OUTTAKES VOL. 9 by Birthday BR 090.

Give Me Some Truth

Written by John.
John: vocals and guitar.
George: lead guitar.
Klaus Voormann: bass.
Andy White: drums.
Rod Linton: acoustic guitar.
Andy Crosswell-Davis: acoustic guitar.
Nicky Hopkins: piano.
Production: John, Yoko and Phil Spector.

'Love'/'Give Me Some Truth'
UK

John was already working on this song during his stay in India. It had not been completed by the time the group recorded the Esher demos. It was not played during the WHITE ALBUM sessions either. We first heard the song during the Get Back Sessions. Here, John played an incomplete version and I will come back to this in the bootleg section.
This song is also known by its work title "Gimme Some Truth".The song was recorded at the A.S.S. studio in July 1971.Although it was originally written in 1968, John gradually changed it so that it became an accusation towards former U.S. president Richard Nixon. John closely followed the Watergate trial and called for the truth to be told. It became the title song for the video/DVD, with the same name, that was released in 2000. John had originally planned to use this track as the title song for the LP, but finally chose the more suitable song "Imagine".

'Love'/'Give Me Some Truth'
UK

Deviating versions of "Give Me Some Truth":
Apart from the version on the IMAGINE LP there are also a number of deviating mixes. The IMAGINE LP has also been released in quadrophony. There is also an 8-track version where each of the 4 tracks can be listened to separately. On the 1987 CD version, the fade out of all the tracks starts earlier than on the vinyl record. The song received another mix for the DVD release of GIVE ME SOME TRUTH.

'Give Me Some Truth'
UK

'Love'/'Give Me Some Truth'
Japan

'Imagine'
Peru

'It's So Hard'
Peru

"Give Me Some Truth" on bootleg

During the sessions for the LET IT BE film, John already recorded a work version. The track is not complete and John clearly still searching for the right lyrics. The oldest known version was recorded on 3 January 1969 and can be found on the bootleg GET BACK JOURNALS 1 by Vigotone VIGO-102, CD2, track 9. It can also be found on the Yellow Dog set THE COMPLETE GET BACK SESSIONS VOL. 3, YDD 005/6, CD1, track 3. John came back to it on 7 January 1969 and played it three times during this session. These versions have been released on the bootleg set GET BACK JOURNALS 2 by Vigotone VIGO-142, CD5, tracks 7, 14 and 15. From the IMAGINE sessions themselves, only an alternate vocal is in circulation. It can be found on the bootleg IMAGINE... ALL THE OUTTAKES by Vigotone VT-188 and THE IMAGINE OUTTAKES VOL. 1 by Birthday BR 015. The IMAGINE film version is on the CD THE IMAGINE OUTTAKES VOL. 6 by Birthday BR 087. There is a quadrophonic mix on THE IMAGINE OUTTAKES VOL. 7 by Birthday BR 088. The recording on the DVD GIVE ME SOME TRUTH can be found on THE IMAGINE OUTTAKES VOL. 8 by Birthday BR 089. This CD also includes the Get Back and home demo versions of this song. Finally, the 5.1 Surround mixes can be found on THE IMAGINE OUTTAKES VOL. 9 by Birthday BR 090.

Oh My Love

Written by John and Yoko.
John: vocals and piano.
George: lead guitar.
Klaus Voormann: bass.
Andy White: drums/tibetian cymbals.
Nicky Hopkins: electric piano.
Production: John, Yoko and Phil Spector.

John and Yoko were going through the healing process of the loss of their child via a miscarriage. This was not the first recording that related to the loss of their child. On the second solo album UNFINISHED MUSIC VOL. 2 LIVE WITH THE LIONS, catalogue number ZAPPLE 01, is the track "Baby's Heartbeat". When they learned that the unborn baby would die, John and Yoko decided to record the baby's heartbeat so that they would at least have some sort of living memory of it. The miscarriage was probably caused by stress because John and Yoko's arrests on 18 November 1968. They were arrested after 219 grammes of marihuana was found at Ringo's house where they had stayed. From the film footage and the photographs it can be seen that it was rather rough. Yoko miscarried on 21 November 1968. Initially, it had been intended to keep the recordings for themselves. It was only when the then relatively unknown Richard Branson asked John for two songs for a flexi disc that was inserted with a student magazine, that John gave him the tape with this track as well as "Two Minutes Silence". Richard Branson was not amused with these tracks and demanded two others, which he never receive.

The legal action, which was due to take place was cancelled on the eleventh hour. Branson started to build his Virgin empire and John and Yoko released their second solo LP. The LP UNFINISHED MUSIC - LIVE WITH THE LIONS was released on 9 May 1969 on the sublabel ZAPPLE. The photograph on the LP cover, which was taken by Susan Wood in room No. 1 of the Second West Ward at Queen Charlotte Hospital in Hammersmith in London, John and Yoko can be seen whilst they are patients at the hospital. Yoko is in bed and John on the ground.

Initially, he had been given an emergency bed, but when it was required for another patient, John decided to sleep on the floor. The LP did not enter the charts, sales of only 5.000 copies is not sufficient to get into the album charts. The song "Oh My Love" was the second attempt to get to terms with this tragic event. John and Yoko quickly started to work on the track. Home demos from 1968 are in circulation on bootlegs. Due to the 'Lost Lennon Tapes' radio shows we have been able to listen to a great deal of

'Instand Karma'/'Oh My Love'
Single CD The Netherlands

'Instand Karma'/'Oh My Love'
Single CD The Netherlands

'Instand Karma'/'Oh My Love'
Single CD The Netherlands

Picture Disc
UK

the rehearsal sessions. These were transmitted on 13 March 1989 in the show 90-12/5 and on 15 July 1991 in the show 91-29/2. From both shows only the first part has been released on bootleg. As the Angry Dog label is now busy releasing the 'Lost Lennon Tapes' in full, it is only a question of time before the missing part is also in circulation.
A video is also going around where a substantial part of the sessions can be seen and heard. Almost 35 minutes of the sessions have been freed that way and released on bootlegs. I will come back to this later on.

Deviating versions of "Oh My Love"

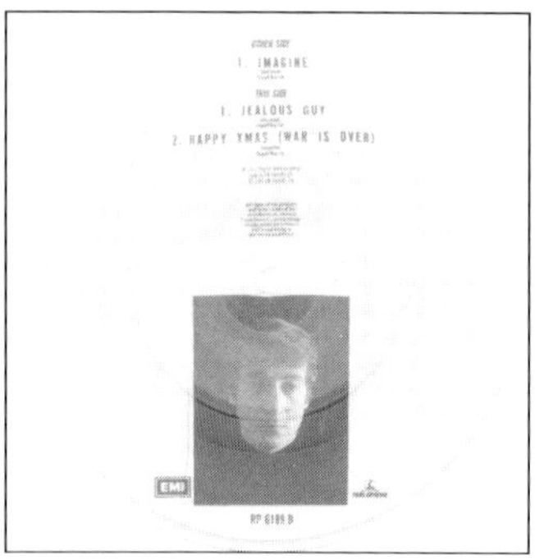

Picture Disc
UK

Apart from the version on the IMAGINE LP, there are also a number of deviating ones.
The IMAGINE LP was also released in quadrophony. There is also an 8-track version where all four tracks can be listened to separately. On the CD version, which was released in 1987, the fade out of all the songs starts earlier than on the vinyl LPs. The song received another mix for the release of the DVD GIVE ME SOME TRUTH. Finally, the IMAGINE CD was reissued in 2000 on CD and vinyl. The recordings were remixed so that everything sounds even clearer than before.

"Oh My Love" on bootlegs

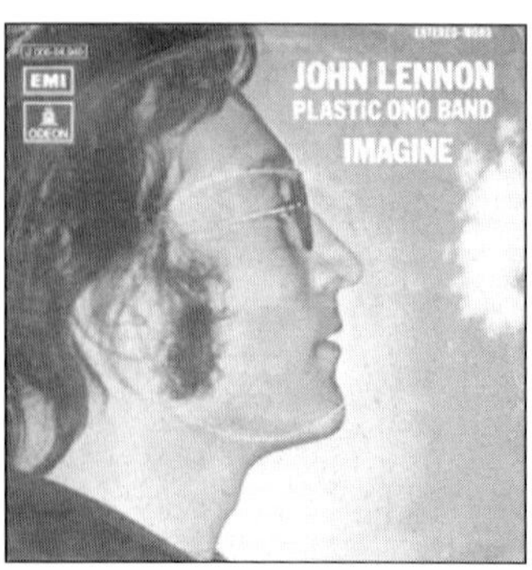

'Imagine'
Spain

As I explained earlier, a substantial part of the recording sessions has come into circulation, both on illegal videos and on LP/CD. For the bootleg collector it is quite simple; if you can not get your hands on the "Lost Lennon Tapes', you will get most of the sessions on the bootleg CD series. These versions have been released on the bootleg set GET BACK JOURNALS 2 by Vigotone VIGO-142, CD5, tracks 7, 14 and 15. There is only one alternate vocal in circulation from the IMAGINE sessions. Take 2 can be found on the bootleg IMAGINE ... ALL THE OUTTAKES by Vigotone VT-188 and THE IMAGINE OUTTAKES VOL. 1 by Birthday BR 015. Alternate takes 1A and B can be found on IMAGINE ... ALL

THE OUTTAKES VOL. 2 by Vigotone VT-189 and THE IMAGINE OUTTAKES VOL. 2 by Birthday BR 016. Two acoustic demos from 1968 can be found on IMAGINE ... ALL THE OUTTAKES VOL. 3 by Vigotone VT-190 and THE IMAGINE OUTTAKES VOL. 3 by Birthday BR 017. The version from the IMAGINE film can be found on THE IMAGINE OUTTAKES VOL. 6 by Birthday BR 087. The quadrophonic version, being the two channel stereo mix from the four channel tape can be found on the CD THE IMAGINE OUTTAKES VOL. 7 by Birthday BR 088. This CD also contains the "Oh My Love" studio sessions that had already been issued on illegal videos before. The recording sessions for the DVD GIVE ME SOME TRUTH are on the CD THE IMAGINE OUTTAKES VOL. 8 by Birthday BR 089.

"Oh My Love" - centre channel.
"Oh My Love" - front channel.
"Oh My Love" - rear channel.

These three recordings are the so-called 5.1 surround mixes that originate from the DVD GIVE ME SOME TRUTH and can be found on THE IMAGINE OUTTAKES VOL. 9 by Birthday BR 090.

'Imagine'
Japan

'Imagine'
Japan

How Do You Sleep?

Written by John, Yoko and Allen Klein.
John: vocals and guitar.
George Harrison: slide guitar.
Klaus Voormann: bass.
Alan White: drums.
Nicky Hopkins: piano.
Not mentioned on the album cover, but played along during the sessions are:
John Tout: acoustic piano.
Rod Linton: acoustic guitar.
Ted Turner: acoustic guitar.
Andy Davis: acoustic guitar.
Producers: John, Yoko and Phil Spector.

'Imagine;
Japan

Without any doubt the most spoken about track from the IMAGINE LP. For the first time ever, one of The

'Imagine'
Japan

'Imagine'
Japan

'It's So Hard'
Japan

Beatles verbally attacked another member of the band. No hidden messages but a frontal assault. If that was not enough, two of the four Beatles played along on this track. Ringo Starr was present during the recording sessions but did not want to beassosiated with it. Why did John put this song on the LP? What caused him to do this? As is often the case, the incident is nothing more than misunderstanding. John believed that several personal attacks were made towards his person on Paul's LP RAM, and decided to fight back. Although it is not credited on the record, some of the lyrics were written by former manager Allan Klein, who still had some old scores to settle with Paul. The RAM LP had only been released one month prior to the start of the IMAGINE recording sessions and both the LP cover and the lyrics infuriated John. On the rear of the sleeve you can observe a couple of beetles ... who are having a good time together. John thought that Paul was insinuating that The Beatles had had it off with eachother. The picture of the two beetles making love appears twice on the back of the LP cover.
John also found various personal attacks on his person in the lyrics of the song "Too Many People" which has the sentence 'Too many people preaching fantasies'. Also the remark about the first and the last mistake were read by John as personal insults.
The song "3 Leggs" was according to John about the lost friendship between himself and Paul. With the 'dog with three legs', Paul is supposed to have meant The Beatles without John. These were actually just opinions of a very frustrated person without any genuine foundation. Only half of the lyrics were written by John, the remainder by Yoko, and as mentioned before, a couple by Allen Klein.

In the book 'Many Years From Now'', published by Beckers & Warburg, ISBN 0-436-28022 1, you can read what Paul told the writer and friend Barry Miles about the events surrounding the song "How Do You Sleep?".

Paul: *'When John did 'How Do You Sleep?', I didn't want to get into a slanging match. And I'm so glad now, particularly after his death, that I don't have that on my conscience. I just let him do it, because he was being fed a lot of those lines by Klein and Yoko. I had the option of going for equal time and doing all the interviews or deciding to not take up the gauntlet, and I remember consciously thinking, No, I really mustn't. Part of it was cowardice: John was a great wit, and I didn't want to go fencing with the rapier champion of East Cheam. That was not a good idea. And I also knew that those vibes could snowball, and you start off with a perfectly innocent little contest and suddenly you find yourself doing duel to the death with the Lennon figure and it's, Oh, my God, what have I carved out here? But it meant that I had to take shit, it meant that I had to take lines like 'All you ever did was "Yesterday".'*

I always find myself wanting to excuse John's behaviour, just because I loved him. It's like a child, sure he's a naughty child, but don't you call my child naughty. Even if it's me he is shitting on, don't you call him naughty. That's how I felt about this and still do. I don't have any grudge whatsoever against John. I think he was a sod to hurt me. I think he knew exactly what he was doing and because we had been so intimate he knew what would hurt me and he used it to great effect. I thought, Keep your head down and time will tell. And it did, because in the Imagine film, he says it was really all about himself.

Flexie Disc
Russia

Flexie Disc
Russia

John about "How Do You Sleep?"

'It's not about Paul. it's about me. I'm really attacking myself. But I regret the association, well, what's to regret? He lived through it. The only thing that matters is how he and I feel about these things and not what the writer or commentator thinks about it. Him and me are okay.'

John later described it as 'using somebody as an object to create something. *I wasn't really feeling that vicious at the time, but I was using my resentment towards Paul to create a song.'*

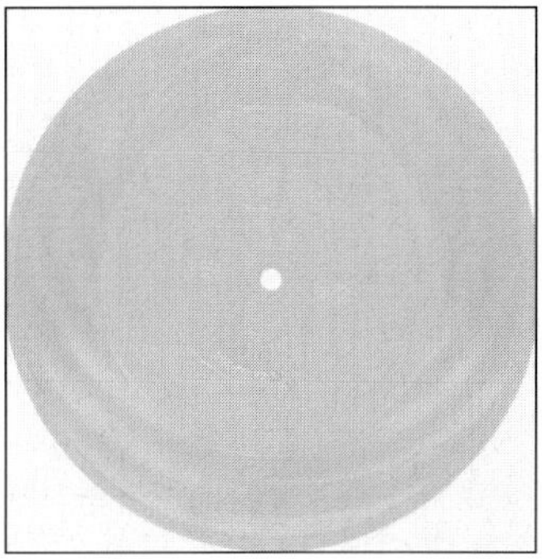

Flexie Disc
Russia

1984 EP release
Russia

John amplified on this explanation in one of his last interviews, recorded for BBC Radio by Andy Peebles two days before he was murdered:
'I used my resentment against Paul that I have as a kind of sibling rivalry resentment from youth, to create a song... rivalry between two guys, I mean, it was always there, it was a creative rivalry, like there was a rivalry between the Beatles and the Stones, it was ... not a terrible vicious horrible vendetta... I used my resentment and withdrawing from Paul and the Beatles and the relationship with Paul to write 'How Do You Sleep?' I don't really go round with those thoughts in my head all the time.

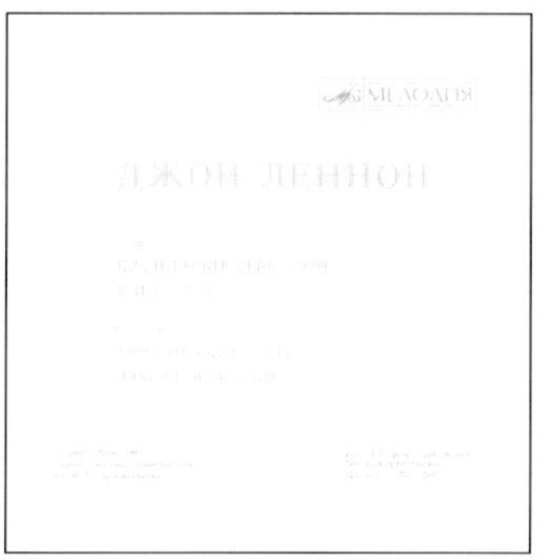

1984 EP release
Russia

In the same book there is also an interview with Felix Dennis, a guest at Tittenhurst during the recording of "How Do You Sleep?".
Felix: 'They were writing the song as they performed it. And as these lyrics emerged, I remember Ringo getting more and more upset by this. He was really not very happy about this, and at one point I have a clear memory of his saying, 'That's enough, John'. There were two magnificent studio musicians, and they too were not very happy about it, but as usual, Lennon plowed his own furrow and he just didn't give a shit whether people liked it or not. It is absolutely true to say that Yoko wrote many of the lyrics. I watched her writing them and then watched her race into the studio to show John - which would often annoy the musicians, but she would race in there anyway, waving a piece of paper and show John she'd had an idea. He would say 'Great' or whatever, and he would add something to it, then he would come back and relax in the control room for a bit and they would confer together. They've both got appalling handwriting, writing in a great hurry.
He would think of a lyric, and then she would think of a lyric, and then they'd burst out laughing, they'd think that was absolutely hysterical. Some of it was absolutely puerile, thank God a lot of it never actually got recorded because it was highly, highly personal, like a bunch of schoolboys standing in the lavato-

1984 EP release
Side A
Russia

ry making scatalogical jokes and then falling about with laughter at their own wit. That was about the level of it but thank goodness in the end somebody obviously talked some sense to them, or they'd talked sense to each other. Maybe Ringo had got onto them and told them not to be so brutal. Some of the lyrics were a lot ruder than you will find on the final version. To counterbalance that, even if it might have been very hurtful to Paul McCartney, I think that the mood in which it was written should be borne in mind, which was one of schoolboy for the hell of it. It's quite obvious that Paul must have been some sort of figure of authority in Lennon's life, because you don't take the piss of somebody that isn't a figure of authority. The mood there wasn't totally vindictive. As I felt it, they were taking the piss out of the headmaster. A lot of giggling, a lot of laughing. They had one line about Paul's Little Richard singing. I don't know if this is true that Paul was always quite proud of his ability to sing like Little Richard; they were making reference to that. It never ended up on the final cut. Phil Spector never said a single word about the lyrics, but Ringo and other musicians there would remonstrate with him and say, 'Oh, for Christ's sake, John, that's a bit too much, you know!' Sometimes he would agree and cross it out. All I can say, if he'd wanted to write something to really hurt Paul's feelings, they certainly compiled enough material to do so. If he'd had someone he could confide in, other than Yoko, I think they would have persuaded him to leave it in the vaults for posterity. It was a bit of a shame he ever let it out.'

1984 EP release
Side B
Russia

1985 EP release
Russia

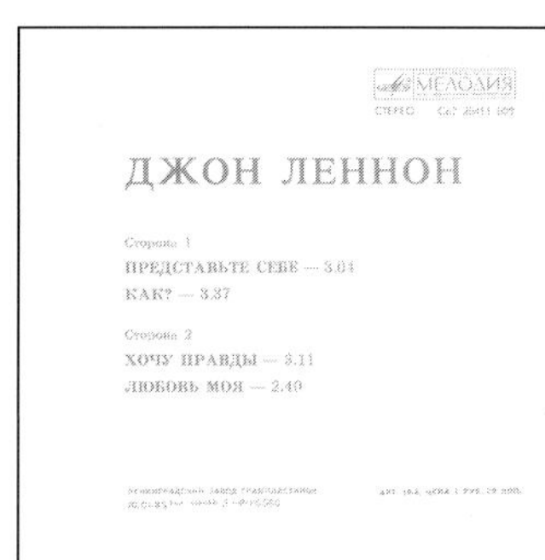

1985 EP release
Russia

Deviating versions of "How Do You Sleep?"

Apart from the version from the IMAGINE LP there are also a number of deviating ones.
The IMAGINE LP has also been released in quadrophony. There is also an 8-track version, where all four tracks can be listened to seperately. On the CD version, the fade out of all the songs starts earlier than on de vinyl LP. The song got another mix for the DVD release of GIVE ME SOME TRUTH.

1885 EP release
Side A
Russia

1985 EP release
Side B
Russia

A deviating mix of the song can also be found on the CD set ANTHOLOGY on CD1 ASCOT, track 15.
My personal opinion has always been that this isYoko's way of giving it another kick. I am convinced that if John would have still been alive that he would not have put this track on the ANTHOLOGY set. Finally, the IMAGINE CD was reissued in 2000 on CD/LP. The recordings were remixed so that everything sounds even clearer than before.

"How Do You Sleep?" on bootleg

A great number of recording sessions of this song have been released on bootlegs. Although they appear on very many compilations, I will restrict my review to the Vigotone and Birthday releases.
An alternate vocal can be found on the bootleg IMAGINE ... ALL THE OUTTAKES by Vigotone VT-188 and THE IMAGINE OUTTAKES VOL. 1 by Birthday BR 015. A total of 9 takes and alternates can be found on IMAGINE ... ALL THE OUTTAKES VOL. 3 by Vigotone VT-190 and THE IMAGINE OUTTAKES VOL. 3 by Birthday BR 017. A very good review about the various sessions, 16 different takes, alternate are on the CD THE IMAGINE OUTTAKES VOL. 4 by Birthday BR 070 and IMAGINE MORE SESSIONS TAPES by Vigotone VT-185/186. We can be hear how this song was constructed. The version from the IMAGINE documentary can be found on THE IMAGINE OUTTAKES VOL. 6 by Birthday BR 087. The quadrophonic version can be found on the CD THE IMAGINE OUTTAKES VOL. 7 by Birthday BR 088. The recordings originating from the DVD GIVE ME SOME TRUTH can be found on the CD THE IMAGINE OUTTAKES VOL. 8 by Birthday BR 089.

How?

Written by John.
John: vocals and piano.
Klaus Voormann: bass.
Alan White: drums.
John Barham: vibes.
Nicky Hopkins: piano.
Producers: John, Yoko and Phil Spector.

This song initially had the work title "How Can I Go Forward?". Just like a great number of the IMAGINE tracks "How?" had already been written at the end of 1969, start of 1970. The recordings which were made in November 1970 have already been released on bootleg CDs. It was written by John in California, when he was living there for a short period. We could first hear these recordings during the 'Lost Lennon Tapes' radio shows. It can be heard that this must have been one of the first occasions that he worked on this song, he still appears to lack direction and during this session which takes place at his home behind the grand piano, the track turns into a work version of "Child Of Nature", also known as "On The Road To Marrakesh". After this very old version of "Jealous Guy" he carries on with the song "Oh Yoko!". This is the third IMAGINE track that can be found on the CD COMPOSITIONS by Vigotone VT-191, in its early work version. I will come back to this . "How?" is in somewhat out of place on the IMAGINE LP. It is a left-over song from the JOHN LENNON AND THE PLASTIC ONO BAND period and John decided to complete it and use it. According to John, George Harrison is supposed to have said that this is the best Lennon number he had ever heard.

'Imagine'
South Africa

'It's So Hard'
South Africa

Deviating versions of "How?"

Apart from the track on the IMAGINE LP, there are also a number of deviating versions.

The IMAGINE LP has also been released in quadrophony. There is also an 8-track version, where all 4 tracks can be listened to separately.

On the CD release from 1987, the fade out of all the

songs starts earlier than on the vinyl LP.
The song was remixed for the DVD GIVE ME SOME TRUTH. Finally, the IMAGINE CD was remixed in 2000 and reissued on CD/LP, so that the recordings sound even clearer than before.

"How?" on bootlegs

As stated above, the oldest home demos of the song can be found on the CD COMPOSITIONS by Vigotone VT-191. These demo recordings can also be found on the nine CD set by Birthday Records THE IMAGINE OUTTAKES, which also includes the first five CDs released by Vigotone with the titles IMAGINE... ALL THE OUTTAKES VOLS. 1 to 3, with the catalogue numbers VT-188, 189 and 190 and IMAGINE MORE SESSION TAPES, VT-185/186. These include the recording sessions for IMAGINE at Tittenhurst Park. Alternate vocals and take 9 can be found on the CDs IMAGINE ... ALL THE OUTTAKES Vol. 1 by Vigotone VT-188 and THE IMAGINE OUTTAKES VOL. 1 by Birthday BR 015. Take 12 and alternate vocals as well as the original take 2 can be found on IMAGINE ... ALL THE OUTTAKES VOL. 2 by Vigotone VT-189 and THE IMAGINE OUTTAKES VOL. 2 by Birthday BR 016. There is a deviating piano version, other than the one on the CD COMPOSITIONS, that can be found on the CDs IMAGE ... ALL THE OUTTAKES VOL. 3 by Vigotone VT-190 and the IMAGINE OUTTAKES VOL. 3 by Birthday BR 017. This CD also includes the medley "How?"/"Child Of Nature"/"Oh Yoko" Although the CDs THE IMAGINE OUTTAKES VOL. 4 by Birthday BR 070 and the first CD of the double CD MORE SESSION TAPES by Vigotone VT185/186 come with the recording sessions of "How Do You Sleep?", they also contain an outtake of "How?". The version used for the IMAGINE documentary can be found on the CD THE IMAGINE OUTTAKES VOL. 6 by Birthday BR 087. Just like with all other IMAGINE tracks, the quad version is on the CD THE IMAGINE OUTTAKES VOL. 7 by Birthday BR 088. The DVD/Video version for GIVE ME SOME TRUTH can be found on the CD THE IMAGINE OUTTAKES VOL. 8 by Birthday BR 089. Finally, THE IMAGINE OUTTAKES VOL. 9 by Birthday BR 090, contains the special 5.1 Surround mixes.

Oh Yoko!

Written by John.
John: vocals, guitar and mouth harmonica.
Klaus Voormann: bass.
Alan White: drums.
Nicky Hopkins: piano.
Rod Linton: acoustic guitar.
Andy: acoustic guitar.
As an extra the duo J & P is mentioned, this is John and Phil Spector, they jointly

did the close
harmonies together.

John wrote the song "Oh Yoko!" during his stay in India. To the outside word, Yoko did not exist and everybody assumed that John and Cynthia were still a happy couple. John missed Yoko badly and expressed this it in this song. A home demo of it was already in circulation at the end of 1968 and was released on the bootleg CD COMPOSITIONS by Vigotone VT-191. The recordings also appear on the IMAGINE OUTTAKES by Birthday Records and I will come back to this. This song had been inspired by the Lonnie Donegan song "Long Lost John". John has played this track himself during the many sessions at his home. The home demo has been released officially by Yoko on the ASCOT CD of the ANTHOLOGY project. The "Oh Yoko!" song was considered one of the most commercial tracks of the LP by EMI/Capitol and a lot of pressure was put on John to release it as a single. John did not want to know anything about it. It was his ode to Yoko and that was that.

Deviating versions of "Oh Yoko!"

Apart from the version on the IMAGINE LP, there are also a number of deviating ones. The IMAGINE LP was also released in quadrophony.

It was also issued as an 8-track where all 4 tracks could be listened to separately. The fade out on the 1987 CD releases starts earlier than on the vinyl LPs.

There is also a deviating version on the video IMAGINE-JOHN LENNON. The song was remixed for the DVD GIVE ME SOME TRUTH. Finally, the IMAGINE album was remixed in 2000 and released on CD/LP with an even clearer sound than before.

"Oh Yoko" on bootlegs:

The most complete home demo version can be found on the CD COMPOSITIONS by Vigotone VT-191. The recordings had already been heard before during the 'Lost Lennon Tapes' radioshows. This version originates from the end of 1968, beginning of 1969.

A number of IMAGINE session takes have been released on the IMAGINE ... ALL THE OUTTAKES and THE IMAGINE OUTTAKES series. I will deal with them, one CD at a time. The demo recordings can also be found on the nine CD set by Birthday Records. "Oh Yoko!" take 9 can be found on the CDs IMAGINE ... ALL THE OUTTAKES VOL. 1 by Vigotone VT-188 and THE IMAGINE OUTTAKES VOL. 1 by Birthday BR 015. Take 7 is on IMAGINE ... ALL THE OUTTAKES VOL. 2 by Vigotone VT-189 and THE IMAGINE OUTTAKES VOL. 2 by Birthday BR 016. A deviating piano mix, which can also be found on the COMPOSITIONS CD is also on the CDs IMAGINE ... ALL THE OUTTAKES VOL. 3 by Vigotone VT-190 and THE IMAGINE OUTTAKES VOL. 3 by Birthday BR 017. On this double CD, there is also a piano and an acoustic demo of the song. The

IMAGINE documentary version can be found on the CD THE IMAGINE OUTTAKES VOL. 6 by Birthday BR 087. The quad version is on the CD THE IMAGINE OUTTAKES VOL. 7 by Birthday BR 088. The "Oh Yoko!" version used for the GIVE ME SOME TRUTH DVD can be found on the CD THE IMAGINE OUTTAKES VOL. 8 by Birthday BR 089. Finally the mix for the 5.1 Surround can also be found on the above mentioned CD.

Tracks that were recorded during the IMAGINE sessions but not released at the time by John:

I'm The Greatest

Written by John.
John: vocals and piano.
During the IMAGINE sessions, John recorded a number of piano demos from which a couple are in circulation. The tracks that were transmitted during the 'Lost Lennon Tapes' radio shows have also been released on the CDs IMAGINE ... ALL THE OUTTAKES VOL. 2 by Vigotone VT-189 and THE IMAGINE OUTTAKES VOL. 2 by Birthday BR 016. A second demo can be found on the bootlegs IMAGINE ... MORE SESSIONS TAPES by Vigotone VT-185/186 and THE IMAGINE OUTTAKES VOL. 4 by Birthday BR 070. Although John had initially planned to record it himself , he believed that it would be better if Ringo sung it rather than himself. Ringo released it on his solo LP RINGO. Various session tapes have been put into circulation over the years. The Lennon version was released officially by Yoko on the CD NEW YORK CITY out of the ANTHOLOGY CD project.

Well (Baby Please Don't Go)

Written by Walter Ward.

Two versions are known about of this track. The first one originates from the IMAGINE recording sessions. An outtake can be found on the bootlegs IMAGINE ... ALL THE OUTTAKES VOL. 1 by Vigotone VT-188 and THE IMAGINE OUTTAKES VOL. 1 by Birthday BR 015. The song had already been recorded at the beginning of the sessions and not a great deal is known about it. We do not know how many takes were made and who exactly played along. We know about John, Jim Gordon on saxophone and Bobby Keys on drums. Finally, the song was not considered to be good enough to be included on the IMAGINE LP and it was shelved. After John's death, Yoko has released it officially on the CD set ANTHOLOGY. The two versions are not identical. The ANTHOLOGY version is a shortened alternate whilst the bootleg versions is complete. The second time John performed a version of the song was during his guest appearance at the Fillmore East Festival in New York, where he played along with Frank Zappa on 6 June 1971.

The song's complete jamming version has been released on bootleg. The best source is the Japanese CD THE FILLMORE TAPES. John released it officially as a shortened version on the double LP/CD SOMETIMES IN NEW YORK CITY.

San Francisco Bay Blues

Written by Jesse Fuller.

The song had originally been released by Ramblin Jack Elliot. Later on, the certain composer Jesse Fuller released his own version. But, the song became wellknown due to a Scott McKenzie. Apart from John, Paul has also performed it. This happened during the television recordings for the programme Unplugged at the Limehouse studios in London on 25 January 1991. Most of this televsion appearance for MTV has been released officially on the numbered limited edition UNPLUGGED (The Official Bootleg). The rendition of "San Francisco Bay Blues" can also be found back on this LP/CD.

A shortened Lennon version was included in show 89-05 of the 'Lost Lennon Tapes', which obviously quickly found its way to various bootlegs.

A completer version can be heard on the bootlegs IMAGINE ... ALL THE OUTTAKES VOL. 2 by Vigotone VT-189 and THE IMAGINE OUTTAKES VOL. 2 by Birthday BR 016.

Discover John...the angry youth, the musician,
the radical, the husband, the father, the lover,
the idealist...through his own words and
personal collection of film and music.
IMAGINE
John Lennon
WARNER BROS
DAVID L. WOLPER ANDREW SOLT "IMAGINE: JOHN LENNON" JOHN LENNON
BUD FRIEDGEN, A.C.E. SAM EGAN SAM EGAN and ANDREW SOLT DAVID L. WOLPER and ANDREW SOLT
R RESTRICTED
ANDREW SOLT

chapter 2

IMAGINE-JOHN LENNON
The Album

IMAGINE-JOHN LENNON
EEC Pressing
Side C

IMAGINE-JOHN LENNON
EEC Pressing
SideD

Once John had died, more and more books about him and Yoko appeared on the market. By itself this was not a problem, many of the books were publi shed by writers who were only in it for the money and quickly threw a book together with the available information. It all changed when the gutter journalist Albert Goldman released his book 'The Lives Of John Lennon'. After first having painted Elvis Presley as a pill swallowing idiot in his Elvis book, it now was John's turn. The attack was hard and without pity. With his book he totally erased the image the fans had about both Elvis Presley and John Lennon. Just like the fans, Yoko Ono was shocked by the book and she decided to go on a contra offensive. Not with interviews in papers and on television, but with a film, a record and book about John. In this chapter I will have a close look at this unique project.

IMAGINE - JOHN LENNON ... the movie.

Yoko called in the help of producer David L. Wolper for making this film. David was an expert in the field of making docume ntaries and had already more than 400 of them to his name before he took on this job. Initially, he had reservations to take on this project with Yoko Ono. It did not appeal to him to be ticked off every so often by Yoko, who would keep strict control of the direction. But, Yoko gave her word that he would have freedom and that she would not interfere with the content of the film. She also promised him that he would get access to the enormous private archive of the Lennons. David decided to risk it and got to work with his producer Andrew Solt. Yoko was true to her word and the doors of the archive were opened and more than 200 hours of film were made available to the film makers. What a job, edit all this, make a film of 90 minutes from such a lot of material. Apart from the films, there were also

Cassette tape
Turkey

IMAGINE-JOHN LENNON
CD

IMAGINE-JOHN LENNON
CD

hundreds of hours of audio tape with recording sessions and interviews. By cleverly making use of the interviews, it was possible to let John tell the story of his live for himself. Images to accompany the interviews could be found from the complete Beatles period as well as the solo era, with exception of the DOUBLE FANTASY sessions. Although there are sufficient images, the directors could not find . They obviously did not search thoroughly as a number of home recordings from the 1979/1980 period hade already gone in circulation illegally. Time was their greatest enemy; the documentary could not be too long and items were constantly added and removed.Thus, the famous appearance on Top Of The Pops, which was recorded on 11 February 1970 and transmitted the following day, was cut out of the film at the last minute due to lack of time.Two different videos were made for this first and also final Top Of The Pops appearance. On the first one, Yoko is holding up banners with instructions and on the second one she is sitting down whilst knitting. The version where she holds up the banners is the best known and has been released officially on the video THE JOHN LENNON VIDEO COLLECTION. The amount of available film footage was overwhelming, not only from sessions, but also real private recordings from in the house, in the kitchen, the bedroom, the bathroom, you name it. The Lennons filmed everything. In the archive was also a complete concert by John in the film 'Rock And Roll Circus'. His version of 'Yer Blues' has been freely available on bootlegs, but the film by The Rolling Stones would only be released on CD and video in 1995. The recordings from 11 December 1968, where John and Yoko were present could not be used in the documentary due to copyright problems relating to the film 'Rock And Roll Circus'. The idea of the film was to tell John's live story, not just about the solo period. Besides using the Lennon archive, assistant Julian Ludwig went on the look-out for film material and audio tapes to fill the gaps in the story. Help was asked from private collectors and radio stations around the

world. Slowly but surely the story took shape and a rough selection was made out of the several hundreds of hours of film. First it was narrowed down to 100 hours, then to 40, then 20 and finally it was reduced to 103 minutes. John had given a great deal of interviews during the final months of his live where he specifically talked about the last 40 years, which was a handy source of information for the producers. The set up was unique, John telling the story about John. John's music fitted perfectly, almost like a jigsaw puzzle, with the dialogue. During their research in the archives, 36 hours of film was found about the IMAGINE sessions. It was decided to show more about these sessions than any other material. The IMAGINE sessions had been filmed very well and were easy to adapt. Not everything went that smooth though. Four hundred hours of film footage plus what had been collected from the outside arrived as 1 and 2" provisional tapes, 16 and 32mm film reels. It is also understandable that the quality varied a lot from film to film. Thus, it was possible that very unique recordings were found that could not be used due to the inferior quality. The producers made a very good job with the section where you can see John and Yoko in bed in Montreal in a heavy discussion with cartoonist Al Capphad. The documentary is made in fullcolour; this was not so with the original images. Capp had a 16mm colour film in his archives where as the Lennons' copy was in black and white. The black and white footage was coloured and fused with the colour film. It is done that well that you will need to look very closely to recognize the section which has been coloured. The differences were not only in the film footage, the same problem ocurred with the sound quality. On several occasions they were forced to replace live recordings with studio versions. The only genuine live recordings in the documentary are the ones from the 'One To One' concerts by John and Yoko from 30 August 1972 at Madison Square Gardens in New York.
More problems had to be solved. The soundtrack had to be adapted. For a record release, the recor-

JOHN LENNON-IMAGINE. CD

'Jealous Guy' Promo CD

'Jealous Guy' Promo CD

'Jealous Guy'
Promo CD

dings are divided over two tracks for stereo. For a film, the sound is divided over three tracks, centre, left and right. George Martin was called to help who used the original mastertapes for this project. Especially the "A Day In The Life" sounds excellent and is the clean version as on the mastertape. Whilst George Martin was given the supervision over the Beatles recordings, producer Rob Stevens started with the solo recordings. There are a total of 36 songs by John and The Beatles which can be heard in this documentary. The film had taken 18 months and costed 6.6 million dollars to make. They were now curious about the reaction by the other Beatles.

The other Beatles watch the film.

The film was virtually completed and they first showed a rough montage to the other Beatles, Yoko and Julian, John's son. Paul watched the film and sung along with most of the songs. The part where John says 'Where do we go?', to the Toppermost of the Poppermost', Paul talked along at the same time, word by word as in the documentary. The producers were obviously curious what Paul's reaction was about the "How Do You Sleep?" section. Notwithstanding the fact that Paul was affected by what he had seen, he did not give any reaction to the wrenched section. His only remark was 'Lennon was a good lad'. George, Ringo and their wives, and Neil Aspinall watched the film together at George's house, where especially the more emotional Ringo was most affected after watching it. George remarked that he found that there was too much Beatles material in the film and this would not give John sufficient credit as a solo performer. Just like for the public, most of the solo images had never been seen before, not even by The Beatles. After Julian had seen the film, he became so emotional that he was unable to talk about it,, it was a very emotional experience for Sean.

Video-CD
China

Video -CD
China

Yoko did keep her word and allowed the producers artistic freedom; just like anyone else she saw the film for the first time when it was screened in its rough version. Although she was not entirely happy with what she had been watching she did not make any changes to the story. If you are watching the documentary, you will be tempted to ask why Paul, George and Ringo do not feature in the film. They were obviously asked, but apart for making available the Beatles images and giving permission to use them, they did not want to be interviewed. Personally, I find this a shame and something that is missing. But, it was their decision and we have to respect this.

Video -CD
China

The film originally had a playing time of 122 minutes and after it was shown to the Warner Bros directors in Los Angeles it was said that it was too long. The producers were told to cut nearly 20 minutes.

Video -CD
China

After a well run advertising campaign where Yoko was present at televsion shows and Beatles and Lennons specials were broadcast on radio and television, the film IMAGINE .. JOHN LENNON was premiered on 6 October 1988 in Manhattan in New York in the presence of Yoko and Sean. The interest by the press was enormous and the documentary received flattering reviews, probably also because it showed footage that had never been seen before. The following day, it was open to the public. All week long special programmes about John were transmitted in the U.S. Fans in Great Britain had to exercise some further patience as the film did not premiere until 28 October 1988 with an advance screening three days earlier. The British premiere took place at the Cannon Cinema in Haymarket in London. Present were, amongst others, Yoko, Cynthia and Sean. Just like in the U.S. it was well received in Europe. After having been shown in the many cinemas around the world, it was finally released on video. At the time of writing this book (November 2002), the film has not yet been released on DVD.

IMAGINE
The book
First print

THE BOOK

"Imagine" became a mega project for Yoko's team. Besides the film, a special book was also published. Just like for the film, the writers got access to the Lennon archive so that photographs were printed which had never been seen befo-re. Just like the film, this became a project by Andrew Solt and Sam Egan. The prologue was written by Yoko and the epilogue by David L. Wolper. The book has 256 pages, is a hardcover edition with a treasure of photographs and the text is composed from interviews by John and Yoko. The reader gets the story first hand just like in the film. The book complements the film. It is a must for all self confessed Lennon and Beatles fan and is written with the same acuracy as the film. It appeared at the same time as the film. In the U.K., the book was released as a hardcover by the publishers Bloomsbury and the retail price at that time was £20. Once the book was sold out, it remained unavailable for a number of years. Fortunately, the Penguin group has reissued it in 1998 as a paperback edition so that this reference book is now also available to the new generation of Beatles fans. To facilitate the search for the book, its catalogue number is ISBN 0-14-027433-2. The book's title is 'Imagine' and the publishers are Penguin Studio.

THE RECORD/CD

Apart from the book and the film, they also released a double LP. It also appeared on CD. For the first time, recordings by both The Beatles and Solo outtakes by John Lennon appeared on the same album.

IMAGINE - JOHN LENNON

Music from the motion picture.

Parlophone PCSP 722 - vinyl - released in the U.K. on 10 October 1988.
Parlophone CD PCSP 722 - CD - released in the U.K. on 10 October 1988.
Capitol C1-90803 -vinyl - released in the U.S. on 4 October 1988.
Capitol CDP-7 90803 2 - CD - released in the U.S. on 4 October 1988.
EMI PM 525 7 91320 1 - vinyl - released in Holland in October 1988.
EMI 164 7 91320 1 - vinyl - released in Holland in October 1988.

Side A:
1) Real Love.
2) Twist And Shout.
3) Help!
4) In My Life.
5) Strawberry Fields Forever.
6) A Day In The Life.

Side B:
7) Revolution.
8) The Ballad Of John And Yoko.
9) Julia.
10) Don't Let Me Down.
11) Give Peace A Chance.

Side C:
12) How?
13) Imagine (rehearsal).
14) God.
15) Mother.
16) Stand By Me.

Side D:
17) Jealous Guy.
18) Woman.
19) Beautiful Boy.
20) (Just Like) Starting Over.
21) Imagine.

In order to get the 21 songs on vinyl it was necessary to release it as a double LP whereas all the songs easily fit on the one CD. There were two genuine new songs on this album, namely the opening song "Real Love" and a rehearsal version of "Imagine".
Another remarkable recording is "A Day In The Life". The song can be heard for the first time with a clean intro without the transfer from "Good Morning, Good Morning" like on the SGT. PEPPER LP/CD.
The LP/CD entered the British album charts on 22 October 1988, reached number 64 and dropped out again after six weeks.

THE SINGLES

In order to draw the attention to the film, and to earn some extra revenue, a single was released.

Great Britain

"Imagine"/"Jealous Guy".
Parlophone R 6199 - vinyl.

Imagine/Jealous Guy/Happy Xmas (War Is Over).
Parlophone CDR 6199 - CD single.

Imagine/Jealous Guy/Happy Xmas (War Is Over).
Parlophone 12R 6199 - 12" maxi single.

All three variations were released on 28 November 1988.
In the U.K. a further variant appeared in the form of a 7" picture disc on 5 December 1988, with the same 2 songs as the 7" single of 28 November 1988, with the catalogue number Parlophone RP 6199.
A 12" picture disc was also planned (12 RP 6199) but was finally not issued.
The single entered the British singles chart and only reached number 45 dropped out of the listings after 5 weeks.

The United States Of America

Jealous Guy/Give Peace A Chance.
Capitol B 44230 - released on 19 September 1988.
Only a vinyl single was issued which did not manage to enter the hit lists.

The Netherlands

Imagine/Jealous Guy/Happy Xmas (War Is Over)
Parlophone 016-2 03089 7.
The single appeared both on vinyl and on CD. It was pressed in Germany, whilst the picture sleeve was printed in The Netherlands.
The CD single has an additional song and was pressed in Holland.

Imagine/Jealous Guy/Happy Xmas (War Is Over)/Give Peace A Chance.
Parlophone CD R6199 - released in 1988.
The single did not enter the Dutch singles charts either.

僕は夢追い人かもしれない　でもそれは僕だけじゃない
いつか君もこの夢を追えば　世界は1つに結ばれるよ
IMAGINE
John Lennon
「イマジン」　ジョン・レノン
Distributed by CABLE HOGUE co., ltd.

john lennon
IMAGINE•THE FILM
The classic music of JOHN LENNON, united with original and unique film of JOHN and YOKO in London, New York and Tokyo.
Imagine
Crippled Inside
Jealous Guy
Don't Count The Waves
It's So Hard
Mrs Lennon
I Don't Want To Be a Soldier
Power To The People
Give Me Some Truth
Oh My Love
How Do You Sleep
How?
Oh Yoko!
60 MINS.
LONDON • NEW YORK • TOKYO

gimme some truth
The Making of John Lennon's "Imagine" Album
imagine john lennon
In the summer of 1971, John Lennon and Yoko Ono went into the studio at their estate in Tittenhurst Park, Ascot, England and recorded the classic album, Imagine. A little known fact is that the Lennons took the unusual step of filming every aspect of the recording sessions. These sessions form the core, heart and soul of Gimme Some Truth - the making of the Imagine album film.

chapter 3

Over the years a number of videos and one DVD have been released with IMAGINE recording sessions.

IMAGINE - THE FILM

EMI-MVP 99 1101 2

Released in November 1985.

Playing time: ca 60 minutes.

1) Imagine.
2) Crippled Inside.
3) Jealous Guy.
4) Don't Count The Waves (Yoko Ono).
5) It's So Hard.
6) Mrs. Lennon (Yoko Ono).
7) I Don't Want To Be A Soldier.
8) Power To The People.
9) Give Me Some Truth.
10) Oh My Love.
11) How Do You Sleep?
12) How?
13) Oh Yoko!

As explained earlier in this book, when John and Yoko started to record the IMAGINE LP in 1971 they decided to film everything so that they could also show the film. The documentary's work title was "Your Show" and it then changed to "Working Class Hero". Apart from the "Let It Be" film this had never been done before. Imagine that the videoclip was still well into the future and music stations such as MTV and VH-1 did not yet exist. The recording sessions of the songs "Oh My Love", "Imagine" and "How Do You Sleep?" were filmed in full. The overdubbing sessions of the songs "Oh Yoko!", "Give Me Some Truth", "How?" and "Jealous Guy" were filmed for the benefit of future generations.

The cameramen were hired who filmed everything on 35mm. For the sound they used a 1/4" Nagra recorder for the soundtrack and for the record they used a multitrack machine. The first number to be filmed was "How Do You Sleep?". It is rather confusing why the Lennons did not do anything with the film footage; they just went into the Lennon archives and nothing surfaced until after John's death.

The video IMAGINE - THE FILM was released in November 1985. From the twenty-three hours of film, images had to be edited for the video release; the correct images where used for most of the recordings, but not with the correct sound. For most of the songs, the officially released tracks from the LP have been used. It would take until 1988 before we would be able to hear the soundtrack from the

film IMAGINE - JOHN LENNON. Again, the images of the recording sessions of IMAGINE were showed but this time with the correct sound. Although the film made an enormous impression on the fans, only a very small amount of the IMAGINE recording sessions was actually shown in this documentary.
The fans got another chance when in 1999, Yoko released a video and DVD with the title GIVE ME SOME TRUTH - THE MAKING OF IMAGINE.

GIMME SOME TRUTH
The Making of John Lennon's Imagine Album.
Capitol 4923483 - video - released in 1999.
Playing time: 63 minutes.

GIMME SOME TRUTH
The Making Of John Lennon's Imagine Album.
Capitol C9RH 492349 - DVD - released in 1999.
For the first time, the recording sessions appeared on DVD as well as on video. The documentary contains the following tracks:

1) Imagine.
2) Crippled Inside.
3) Oh Yoko!
4) Jealous Guy.
5) It's So Hard.
6) I Don't Want To Be A Soldier Mama.
7) Gimme Some Truth.
8) Oh My Love.
9) How Do You Sleep?
10) How?
11) Imagine.
12) Film Credits.

The video has a playing time of 63 minutes, but the DVD comes with a number of extras:

1) Album Discography with audi samples.
2) Chapter Selection.
3) Dolby Digital 5.1 surround sound and stereo.
4) John and Yoko interview.
5) English subtitles for the documentary.
6) 8-page booklet containing rare photographs and backgrounds to the making of 'Gimme Some Truth'.

Nearly thirty years after it was actually filmed, the public finally got what had been intended, a film documentary about the making of the IMAGINE LP.
The fans obviously are always on the look-out for more images from the recording sessions. The DVD is only one hour long and there are 35 hours of film!
The question is whether these images will ever see daylight, some of them are in circulation illegally such as about half an hour of the "Oh My Love" sessions. The quality is never very good but if gives a good idea about the way used to get about his work.
We just will have to wait for new documentaries and hope that other images will be used. The recordable DVD is now on the market, and it will not take very long before the sessions that are in circulation amongst fans privately, will find its way onto the market.

chapter 4

JUST IMAGINE

AT ABOUT 12.30 am on a heavy Wednesday evening, recently someone laid an album on a heavy room of people. It broke the night air that had trespassed on the party.

Roy Hollingworth previews JOHN LENNON'S new album

Evil

After two years of failing to understand a personal idol, John Lennon, it all slipped into place, became clear, and at times venomously evil. I just couldn't believe this new Lennon album. Simply titled "Imagine," it is due for release at the end of September.

With the exception of "Cold Turkey," which for unknown reasons cut its way cleanly into my head, the other Lennon "diaries" had hit me like varied pieces of a jigsaw, musically, and lyrically. I couldn't get moved by it, felt low, damned low. It was inconceivable that a figure I had loved so dearly could suddenly fail to fire any emotion. Forced, and at times, strained optimism, kept the memories in an insecure state of cold storage. Maybe they'd be added to, maybe.

We need evil songs. We need songs of such guts and turmoil to keep the mind striving. For the first time in two years Lennon made me clench my fist, and grit my teeth, and raise a bowed head. This is an incredible Lennon album, an album that has already paled McCartney, Harrison and Starr into a living, but watercolour backdrop.

The first surprise was the return of Lennon to weaving, melodic vehicles, captured and magnified by recognisable, but not obvious Phil Spector treatment. It's laid sweetly on the ear, and obviously one's impulses are tricked by Lennon first, and then what surrounds it. It wasn't until we were about halfway through the first side that I realised how beautiful Spector's treatment was. From then on the ear takes in all, Lennon became not a man on a precarious preaching edge, but a musician with an awful lot of music and a bulging warbag of things to say.

Complex

Musically the first track brought a "Whiter Shade of Pale" feeling to the chord changes. It's a far more complex Lennon, but even then the songs retain the somewhat earthy, basic score. It's increasingly hard to put together smooth reading, having only heard the album once. I can only go by first impressions, and apart from the more musical side, this is also a percussion album.

Alan White's drumming is magnificently recorded, and there's a well-defined emphasis on simple "damp" delivery making for solid, complete packages. Lennon also seems to have finally perfected (for me anyway) that harsh, steel rock 'n' roll treatment. It's so rasping, and gutsy, and one of these outings in particular is ridiculously commercial.

Vocally Lennon appears stronger and more at home, biting and getting that back of the throat grit—something he has never neglected—but just wait to hear him now.

Bitter

"So you thought you were surprised with Sgt. Pepper" are the opening lines to the most cutting article I've ever heard from Lennon. It appears as a strong, bitter put down of McCartney with few holds barred. There's references to "that pretty face," and people saying that "Yesterday" was the "only thing we'd done." How does one take that? As a track it's evil, pushing, and reflective. Lennon's songs are diaries, and obviously McCartney figures in more than a few entries.

Melody Maker October 1971

JOHN LENNON'S "Imagine," already the number one album in America, shot up the MM LP chart to number 5 this week.

Simultaneously, in New York, John and the Plastic Ono Band were recording a new single, for release just before Christmas.

John and Phil Spector were also mixing down tapes of the Plastic Ono Band's gig at London's Lyceum last year, and of John's recent appearance with Frank Zappa at Fillmore East, New York.

These will be issued by Apple as an album called "London Air And New York Wind," around Christmas-time.

The MM was in New York to watch the sessions. An exclusive report begins on page 26.

Melody Maker
November 1971

Pop goes Lennon . . . and he's great

IT'S amazing how much improvement there is on a musician/musicians' album when he/they do not feel he/they have to prove anything. It's also amazing how much we expect from that type of musician/musicians as listeners. John Lennon reached my expectations with "IMAGINE" (Apple PAS 10004, £2.15) and produced one of the best if not *the* best and most enjoyable albums of the year.

John Lennon is a working class hero of today concerned with his problems of today. But for all that he has packed them with fine music and lyrics that entertain as well. Some of the songs have built in obsolescence about them but the majority are timeless and memorable and very unlike the Lennon we have come to know and love or hate or laugh at.

by GAVIN PETRIE

IMAGINE (2.59) John Lennon—piano; Klaus Voorman—bass; Alan White—drums.

A slow ballad, soft pedalling on the piano with strings and a powerful melody line. The lyrics are an incitement to anarchy or a new deal for the world, depending how you feel.

CRIPPLED INSIDE (3.43) John Lennon—guitar; Klaus Voorman, Steve Brendell — upright basses; George Harrison—Dobro; Nicky Hopkins—piano; Ted Turner, Rod Linden and John Tout—acoustic guitars.

A honky tonk song that bounces along, throwing in lots of musical cliches just for fun. Delightful lyrics getting straight to the point. One that the country pickers from Nashville or Val Doonican will latch on to quickly.

JEALOUS GUY (4.10) John Lennon—guitar; Klaus Voorman—bass; Jim Keltner—drums; John Barham—harmonium; Alan White—good vibes (?)

Slow rocker, heavy with strings and a strong melody with weepy lyrics. The song could have come from "Rubber Soul."

IT'S SO HARD (2.22) John Lennon—guitar; Klaus Voorman—bass; Jim Gordon—drums; King Curtis—sax.

A white R-n-B sound with a harsh John Lennon guitar that is very much his, or at least the Plastic Ono Band's sound. Overlaid rather surprisingly with strings and a wailing rock-n-roll sax.

I DON'T WANNA BE A SOLDIER—I DON'T WANNA DIE (6.01) John Lennon—guitar; Klaus Voorman — bass; Jim Keltner—drums; George Harrison—slide guitar; Nicky Hopkins—piano; Badfinger's Joey and Tommy—acoustic guitars; Mike Pinder—tambourine; Steve Brendell—maracas; King Curtis—saxes.

A real Plastic Ono sound with that heavy effect as if the band were busking in an underground station. The negative lyrics are really just there to carry a fat sound.

GIMME SOME TRUTH (3.11) John Lennon—guitars; George Harrison—lead; Klaus Voorman—basses; Alan White—drums; Rod Linton and Andy—acoustic guitars; Nicky Hopkins—piano.

Large whack of Lennon at his best, closely resembling the "Polythene Pam" era of music and lyrics with that harsh, aggressive, distainful Lennon voice. Heavy, fat sound with the mantra-like Harrison lead guitar all the way through. It's the sort of song you would expect to contain more "colourful" language from Lennon, but he restrains himself.

OH, MY LOVE (2.40) John Lennon—piano; Nicky Hopkins — electric piano; Klaus Voorman—bass; Alan White — drums, Tibetan cymbals; George Harrison—guitars.

A beautiful melody and lyric with Lennon almost dropping his defences and being gentle and loving. A soft, slow love song.

HOW DO YOU SLEEP? (5.29) John Lennon—guitar; George Harrison—slide guitar; Klaus Voorman—bass; Alan White—drums; Nicky Hopkins—piano.

A rolling song with stuttering, but driving beat and almost certainly lampooning McCartney with lyrics like "those freaks was right when they said you was dead." Very bitter.

Great, but all too short slide guitar solo from George.

HOW? (3.37) John Lennon—piano; Klaus Voorman—bass; Alan White—drums; John Barham—vibes; Nicky Hopkins—piano.

Seemingly a parody of "Long And Winding Road" heavy with strings just to lay on the sarcasm a bit heavier.

OH, YOKO! (4.08) John

Lennon—guitar, mouthorgan; Klaus Voorman—bass; Alan White—drums; Nicky Hopkins—piano; Rod Linton and Andy—acoustic guitars. Plus the J and P Duo.

A bouncy, up-tempo rock-n-roll number with delightful sentiments John sings like a shy five-year-old professing his love.

LENNON 'SUPERALBUM' REVIEWED

John is back in Beatle form

JOHN LENNON: 'IT'S THE ASCOT SOUND'.

Mike Hennessey reviews 'Imagine'

JOHN LENNON – and wife Yoko – regard his new album, "Imagine," as better than anything he has ever done before.

And they are right.

John, who describes his songs as "electric 20th century folk music" has put together ten tracks which are full of melodic and lyrical interest and which match some of the great songs he wrote before the break-up of the Beatles.

The title track Lennon feels has the best lyric of all the songs on the album; but all the tracks have merit and "Jealous Guy" and "How" in particular are likely to create a lot of attention.

The tracks were all recorded in John's own studio in his Ascot home ("Ascot sound" he calls it) with strings dubbed in later in New York. Four of the tracks were recorded in quadrasonic.

Musicians on the tracks included George Harrison, Alan White, Jim Gordon, Jim Keltner, Nicky Hopkins and Klaus Voormann. Lennon says he would also have used Ringo on drums but he was away filming in Spain.

The music on the album is basically simple – but makes compulsive listening.

IMAGINE: opens the album with a simple piano introduction and John comes in with a wistful vocal, "Imagine there's no heaven . . ." The song has a good hook in a repeated two-bar phrase on the chords of D minor, G seventh, C and E seventh.

'electric twentieth century folk music'

CRIPPLED INSIDE: also in the key of C, is a rocking, countryish piece with jangling piano and an old-time coda descending in half-steps to A7 for a real music hall ending. But the lyric is typically sardonic Lennon. "You can wear a mask and paint your face, you can call yourself the human race, you can wear a collar and a tie, but one thing you can't hide, is when you're crippled inside . . ." A powerful song.

JEALOUS GUY: Lennon wrote this tune originally when he was in India. It was intended as a send-up of the old "Desert Song" type of ballad about sheiks and burning sands. (Sample lyric: "On the road to Marrakesh, I was dreaming more or less . . ."). But when he played it to George Harrison and Phil Spector "their faces dropped." So he changed the style slowed the tempo and came up with what is a very fine ballad.

IT'S SO HARD: This is a rollicking eight-to-the-bar near-blues in A with some wailing guitar that sounds like George.

I DON'T WANT TO BE: Very much in the mood and style of "I Found Out," this is a percussive piece in A minor. It is the longest track on the side and deals with a man who doesn't want to be a soldier, doesn't want to die.

GIVE ME SOME TRUTH: Another powerful, cynical song with a virulent lyric that condemns "short-haired, yellow-bellied, neurotic, psychotic politicians" and "up-tight, short-sighted, narrow-minded hypocrites." Strong on both lyric and music.

OH MY LOVE: Written jointly with Yoko, this is a pleasant ballad with a simple but effective piano backing.

HOW DO YOU SLEEP: John's fondness for songs which mention other songs makes itself felt here with a reference to "Sergeant Pepper." Also reminiscent of "I Found Out," it has a simple rhythmic backing of straight four-in-the-bar cymbals and a five-note guitar riff behind the vocal.

HOW: This is one of the best songs on the album, with another wistful lyric that asks "How can I go forward when I don't know which way I'm facing . . . How can I give love when I don't know what it is I'm giving?" There is an echo from "Long And Winding Road" in the five syncopated stab chords after certain phrases in the lyrics. A typical Beatle song.

'short-haired yellow-bellied'

OH YOKO: A brisk, lively number with wailing harmonica, which shifts between B flat minor and D flat (although it could be A minor and C speeded up!). It's a happy tribute from John to Yoko . . . "In the middle of the night I call your name . . . my love will turn you on." . . . with a chorus "Oh Yoko" in harmony rather reminiscent of "Three Blind Mice."

"Imagine" is going to be a runaway success. It is far and away the best solo album John has done.

ANOTHER impressive artistic achievement by John Lennon is the twenty-minute colour film, "Erection" – a superbly alluring title for what is an entirely non-salacious production.

"Erection" is a cleverly

AND A TWENTY MINUTE ERECTION

conceived movie created from stills, shot over a period of 18 months, of a hotel being built opposite the West London Air Terminal. It starts will the basic foundation on the empty site and finishes with the complete building.

The film was shot entirely from one vantage point, yet by clever use of fading techniques and superimposition, it holds the interest from start to finish and creates a mesmeric fascination as scaffolding appears and disappeares in seconds, lorries arrive and vanish without trace and steel erectors seem to make giant leaps across the girders.

The soundtrack, by Yoko Ono, involves a completely non-melodic use of the human voice with tinkling strings in the background; yet it is strangely effective and apposite.

"Erection" will certainly enhance John's reputation as a creative film maker when it is shown at the Edinburgh Festival.

Record Mirror
1971

Record Mirror
October 1971

imagine
john
lennon

Imagine-USA

It's So Hard - USA

Imagine -UK

IMAGINE-EP Mexico

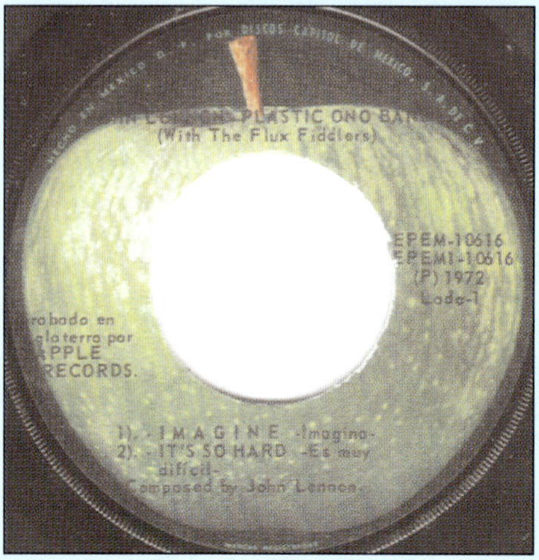

IMAGINE EP -Mexico

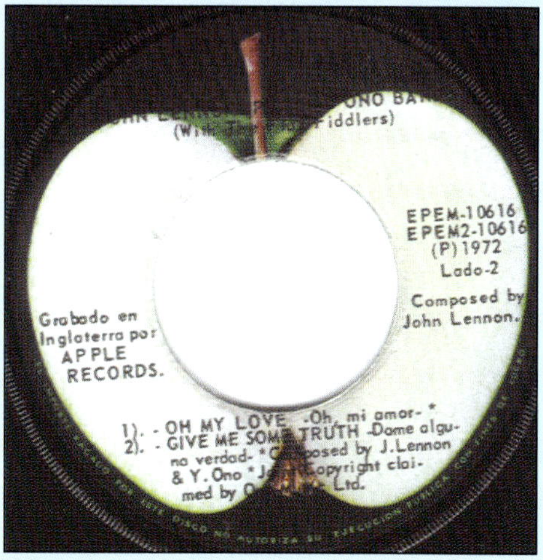

IMAGINE EP - Mexico

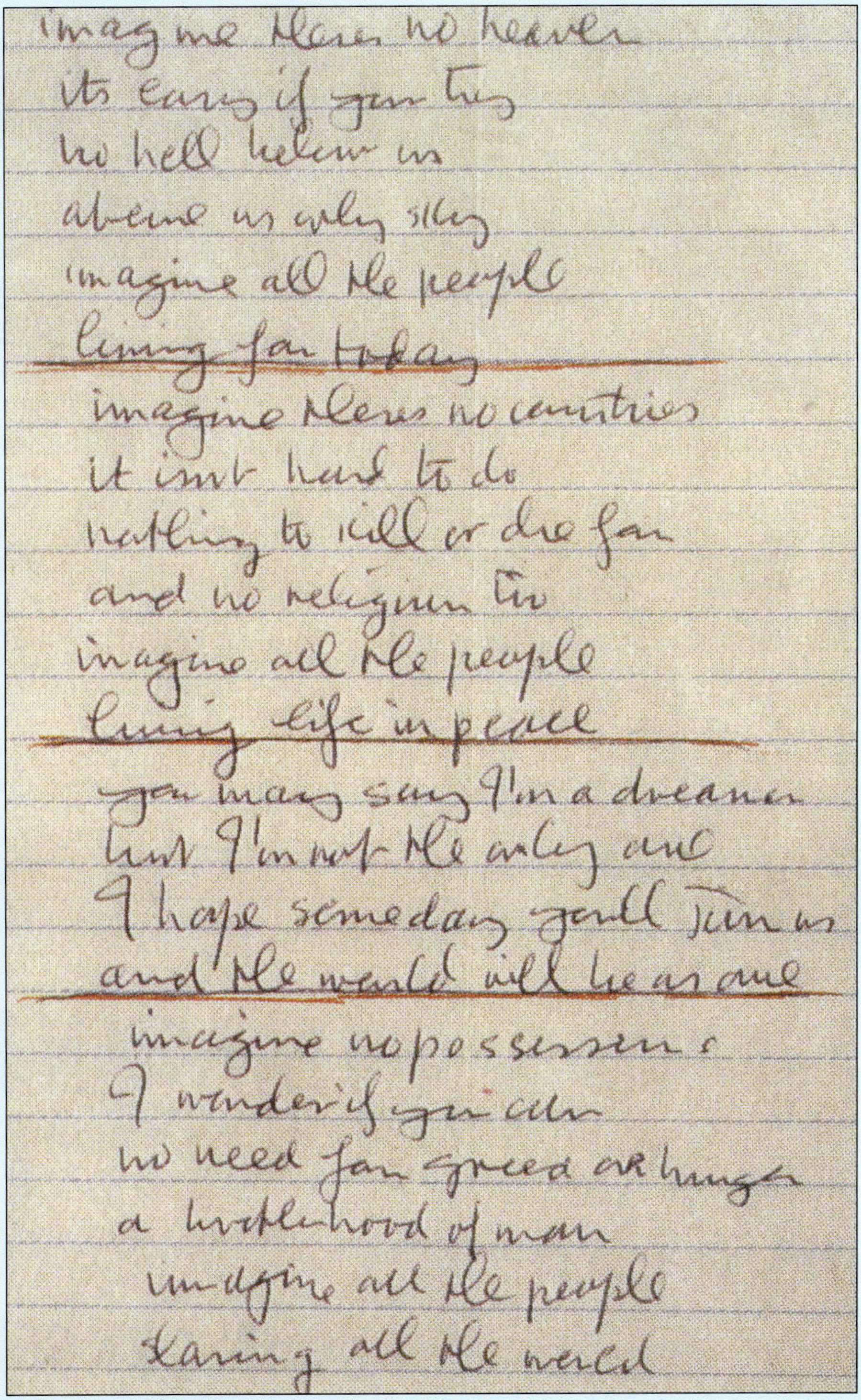
imagine theres no heaven
its easy if you try
no hell below us
above us only sky
imagine all the people
living for today

imagine theres no countries
it isnt hard to do
nothing to kill or die for
and no religion too
imagine all the people
living life in peace

you may say I'm a dreamer
but I'm not the only one
I hope someday youll join us
and the world will be as one

imagine no possessions
I wonder if you can
no need for greed or hunger
a brotherhood of man
imagine all the people
sharing all the world

text 'Imagine'

Germany (front)

Germany back (1st release)

Germany (back -second release)

Germany - rerelease

Germany sleeve

Germany

Germany 12 inch (sealed)

Germany 12 inch

Germany 12 inch

Germany 12 inch (second release)

Germany 12 inch (second release)

Germany

France (front)

France (back)

France

France

Peru

Peru

Italy (front)

Italy (back)

Italy

Spain

South Africa

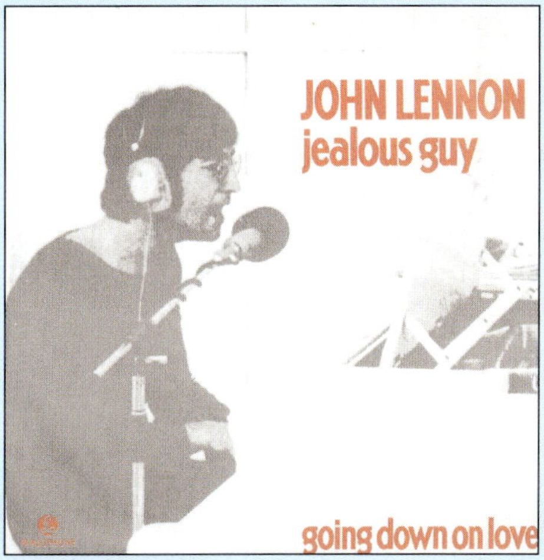

The Netherlands

Russia flexidisc

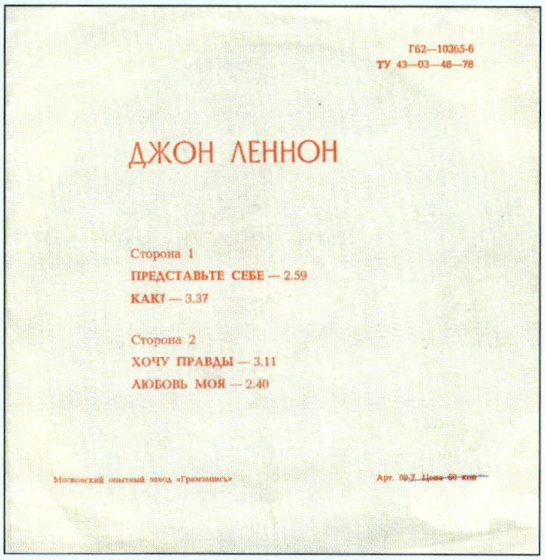

Russia flexidisc

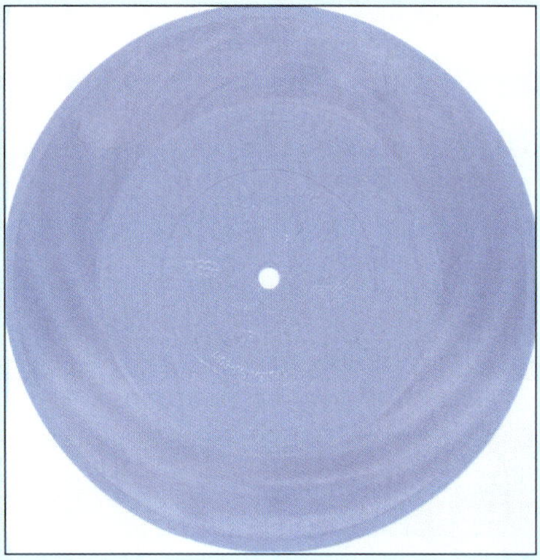

Russia flexidisc

Russia IMAGINE EP (front)

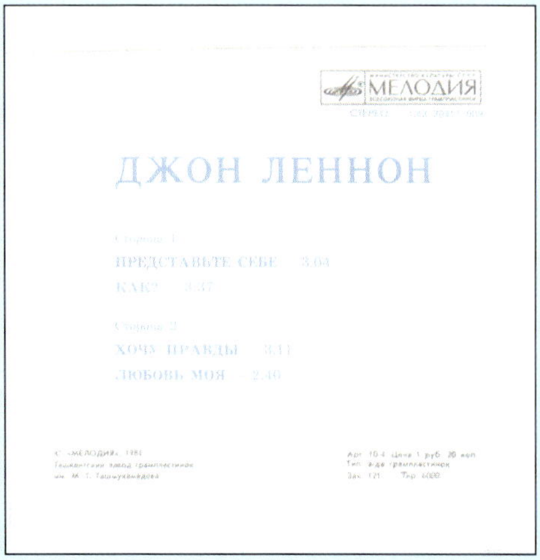

Russia IMAGINE EP (back)

Russia IMAGINE EP

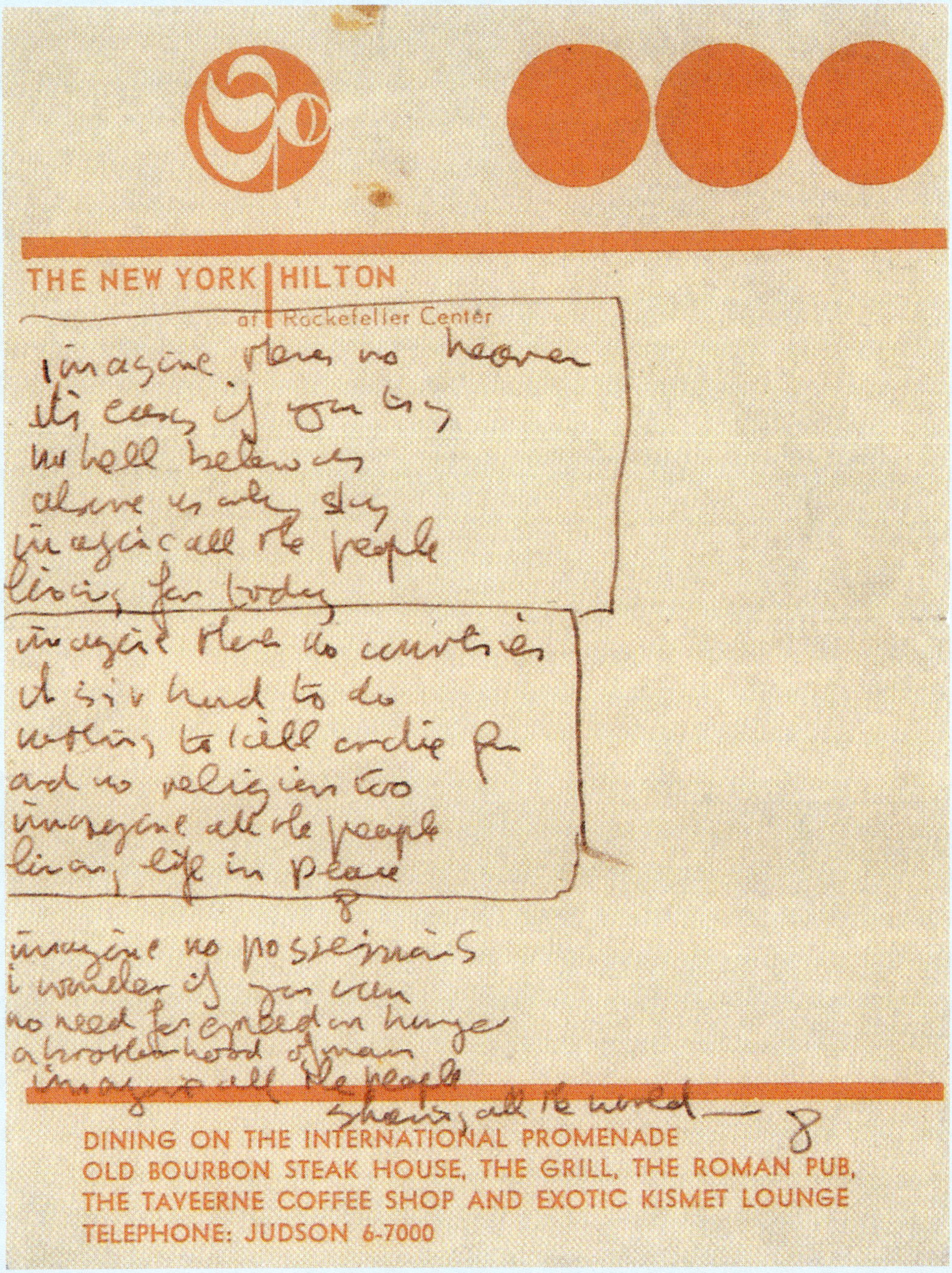

THE NEW YORK HILTON
at Rockefeller Center

imagine there's no heaven
its easy if you try
no hell below us
above us only sky
imagine all the people
living for today

imagine there's no countries
it isn't hard to do
nothing to kill or die for
and no religion too
imagine all the people
living life in peace

8

imagine no possessions
i wonder if you can
no need for greed or hunger
a brotherhood of man
imagine all the people
sharing all the world — 8

DINING ON THE INTERNATIONAL PROMENADE
OLD BOURBON STEAK HOUSE, THE GRILL, THE ROMAN PUB,
THE TAVEERNE COFFEE SHOP AND EXOTIC KISMET LOUNGE
TELEPHONE: JUDSON 6-7000

2nd text 'Imagine'

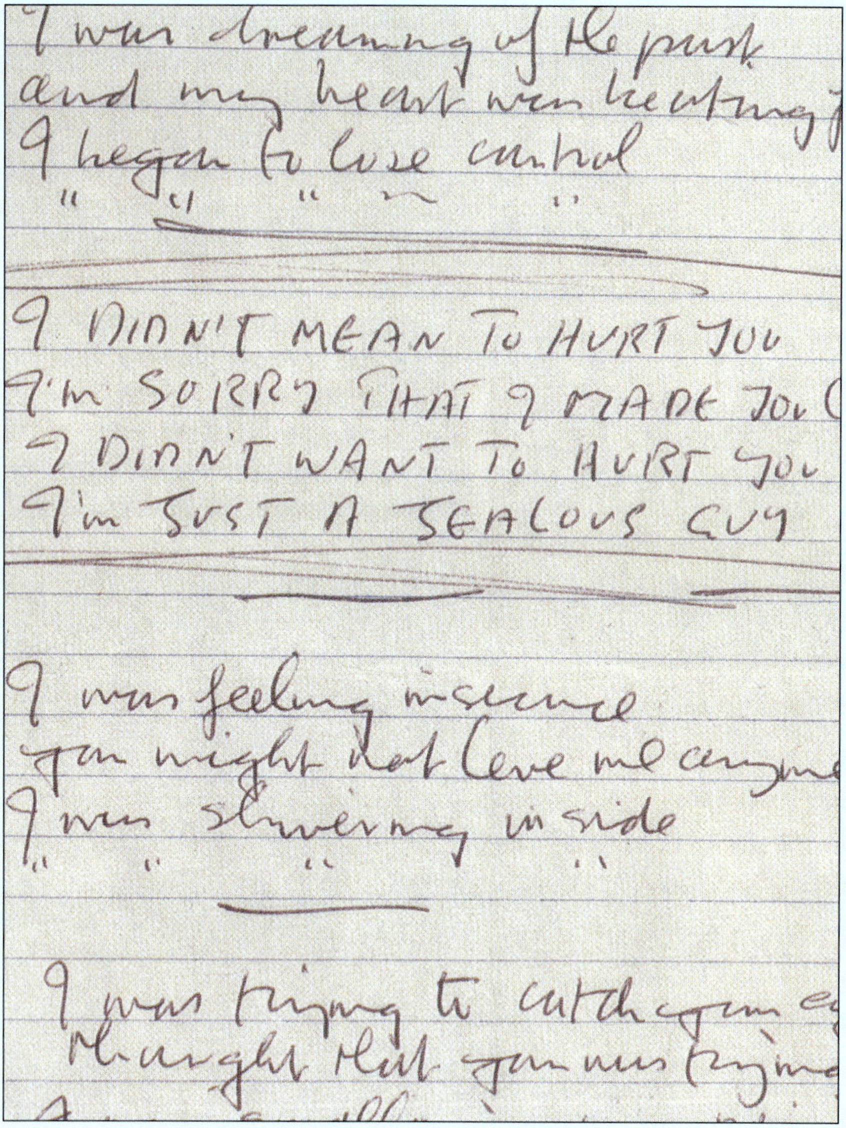
I was dreaming of the past
and my heart was beating f
I began to lose control
" " " " "

I DIDN'T MEAN TO HURT YOU
I'M SORRY THAT I MADE YOU C
I DIDN'T WANT TO HURT YOU
I'M JUST A JEALOUS GUY

I was feeling insecure
you might not love me anymo
I was shivering inside
" " " "

I was trying to catch your e
thought that you was trying

'Jealous Guy' text

Japan (front)

Japan (back)

Japan

Japan

UK

UK

UK Picture disc

UK Picture disc

Jealous Guy -Brazil

Jealous Guy - France (front)

Jealous Guy - France (back)

Jealous Guy - France

Gimme Some Truth DVD (USA) and video (Europe)

Taiwan

Taiwan

Russia (first release)

Russia (second release)

Russia (back)

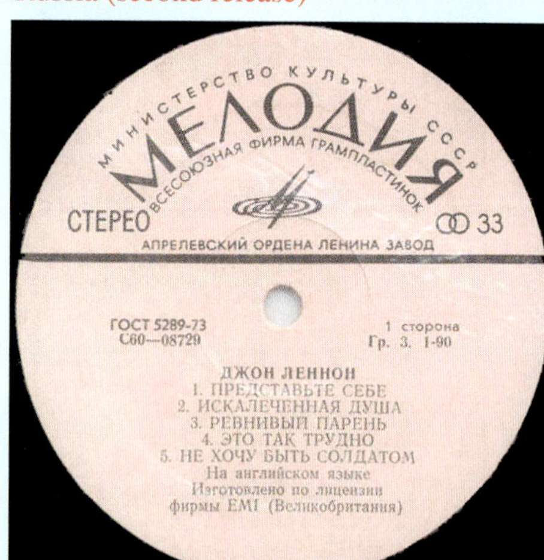

Russia (second release)

Quadrophonic -Germany

Quadrophonic -Germany

Quadraphonic -Germany

Quadraphonic 8-track-USA (1st.release

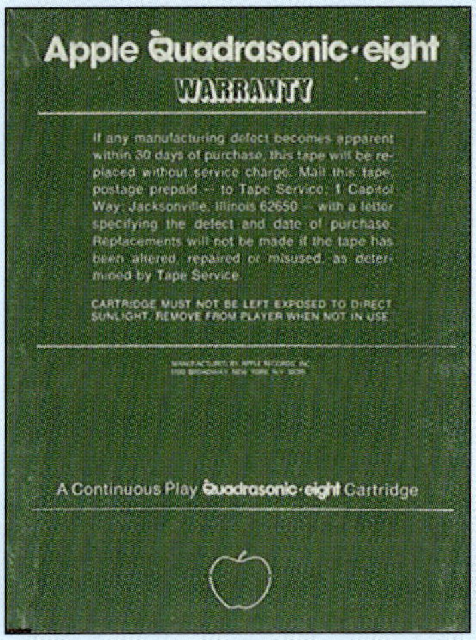

Quadraphonic 8-track-USA (1st.release

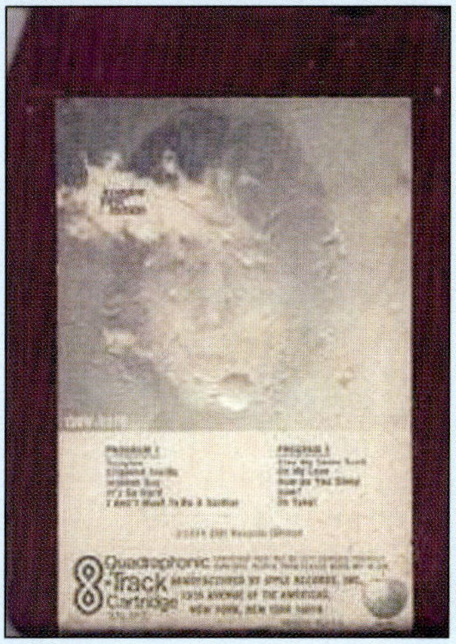

Quadraphonic 8-track-USA (2nd .release

8-track - Germany

LENNON Boxset Greece

Cassette Tape- The Netherlands

Reel to reel - USA

Halfspeed Master - USA

Halfspeed Master - USA

Promoflyer - Japan

Japan ~(first release)

Japan (first release)

Japan first release)

Japan

Japan

UK 2000 rerelease

UK 2000 rerelease

UK 2000 rerelease

UK 2000 rerelease

UK (first release)

UK Quadrophonic

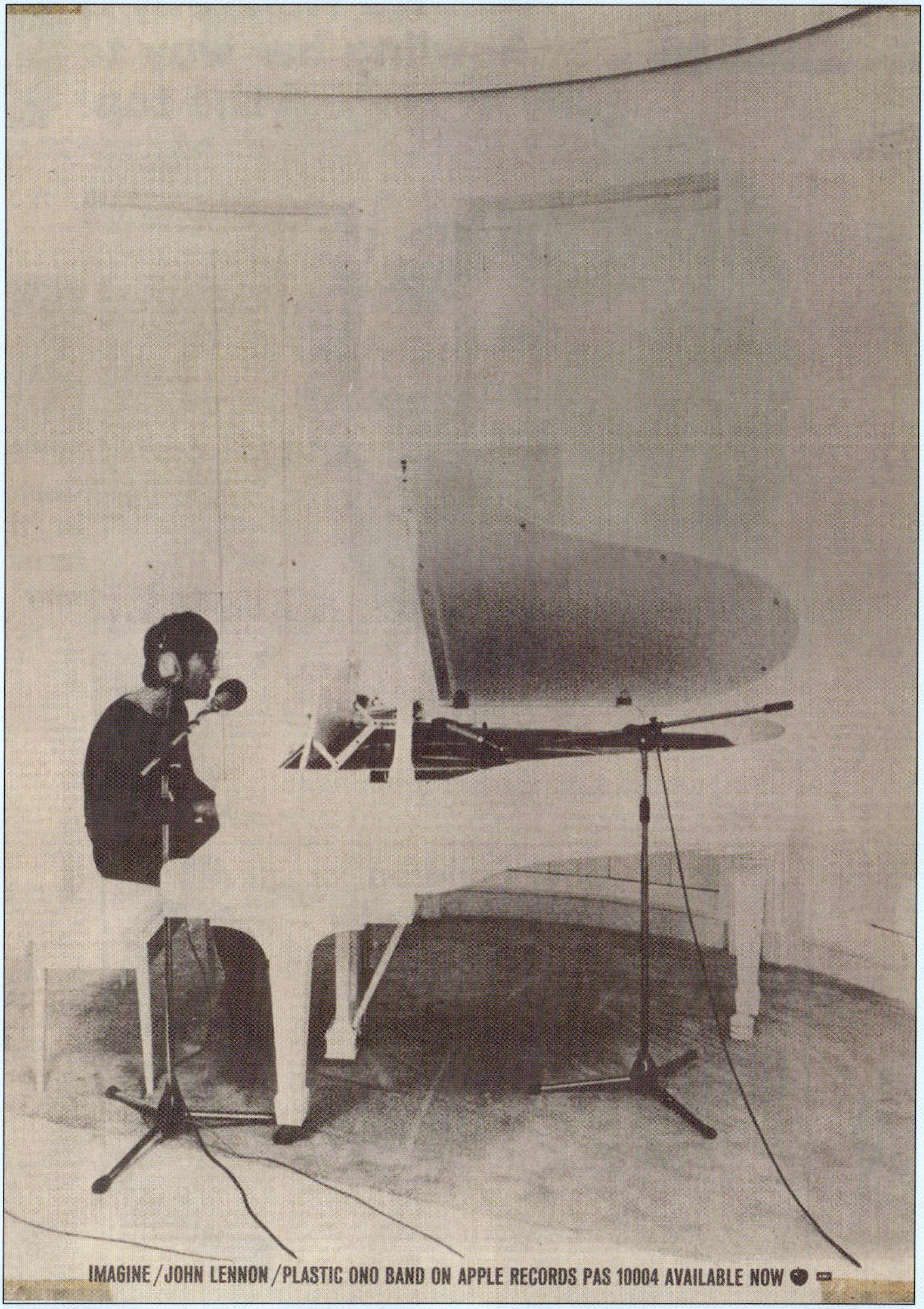

Advert IMAGINE

Promolabel Brazil

Promo CD France (front)

Promo CD France (back)

Promo CD France

LENNON COLLECTION USA Promo

Jealous Guy USA Promo single

ANTHOLOGY Promo (front)

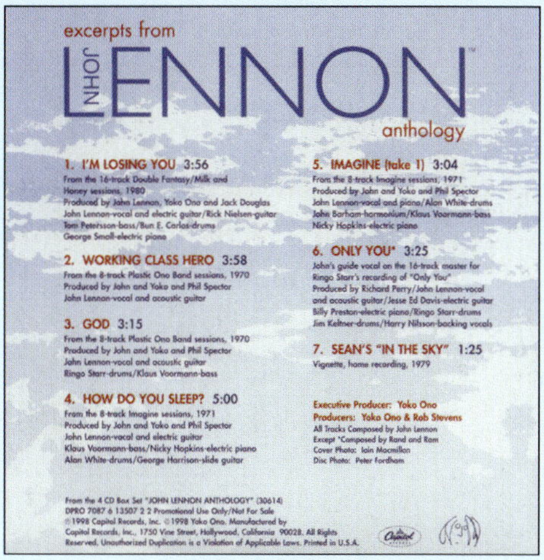

ANTHOLOGY Promo (back)

ANTHOLOGY Promo CD

EMI 100 YEARS Promo set

EMI 100 YEARS Promo CD

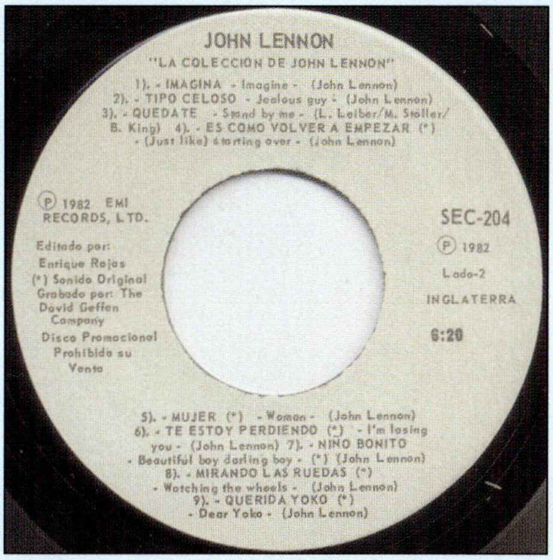

Medley Promo-Mexico

Jealous Guy Promo CD (front)

Jealous Guy Promo CD (back)

Jealous Guy Promo CD

LEGENDS Promo CD)

LEGENDS Promo CD

LEGENDS Promo CD

IMAGINE Selections Promo CD (front)

IMAGINE Selections Promo CD (back)

IMAGINE Seletions Promo CD

STARTING OVER Promo CD (front)

STARTING OVER Promo CD

UK Single Promo (front)

UK Single Promo (back)

UK Single Promo CD

IMAGINE Acetate

SHAVED FISH (Golden Award)

Denmark

Testpressing Israel

IMAGINE - Australie

IMAGINE -Bulgaria

IMAGINE Canada

IMAGINE The Netherlands

Russia (first release)

FRANCE

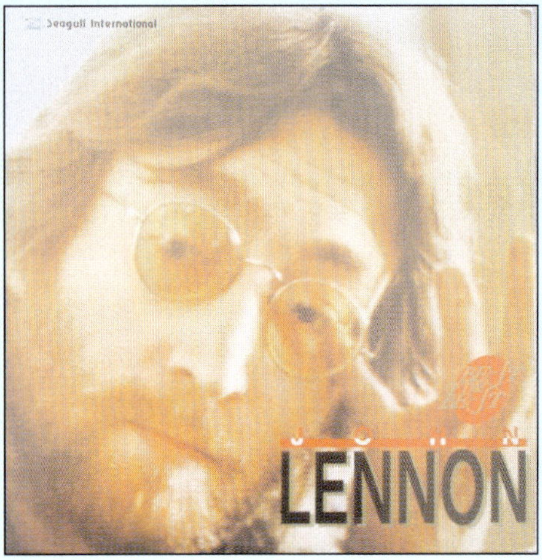

Korea (front)

Korea (back)

Video CD China (front)

Video CD China (inlay)

Video CD China

Video CD China

'Imagine' Music postcard Polland

UK (picture disc)

UK (picture disc)

Japan

SHAVED FISH Japan

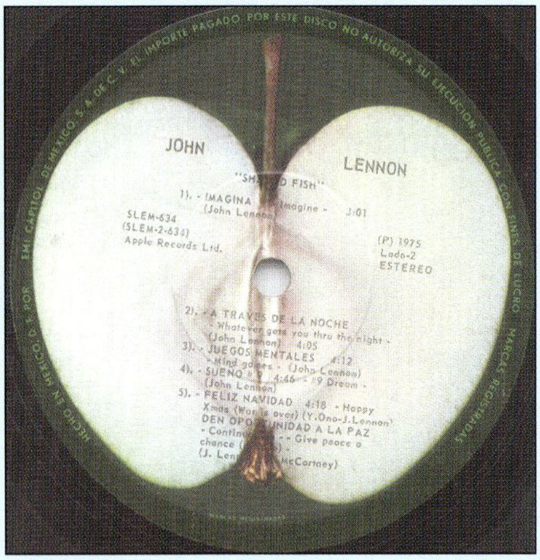

SHAVED FISH Mexico

SHAVED FISH East Germany

SHAVED FISH India (front)

SHAVED FISH India

SHAVED FISH Israel (detail)

Israel

ANGEL BABY vinyl bootleg

Bootleg Picturedisc A

Bootleg Picturedisc B

TELECAST Bootleg Picturedisc

HOUND DOG vinyl bootleg

JOSHUA TREE TAPES Vinyl bootleg

All The Outakes - Vigotone boxset

All The Outtakes Vigotone CD 1

All The Outtakes - Vigotone booklet

All The Outtakes - Vigotone CD 1

THE IMAGINE OUTTAKES VOL.1

THE IMAGINE OUTTAKES VOL.1

THE IMAGINE OUTTAKES VOL. 6

THE IMAGINE OUTTAKES VOL. 7

THE IMAGINE OUTTAKES VOL. 8

THE IMAGINE OUTTAKES VOL. 9

Movie poster

chapter 5

The Album and the singles and Retrospective releases of IMAGINE

IMAGINE
UK

In this review I will indicate which various LPs and singles have been released over the years, the release dates of the IMAGINE LPs and CDs and tracks which originate from this alnum. In the review I will list what has been released in Great Britain, United States Of America, Japan and The Netherlands.

GREAT BRITAIN

IMAGINE
USA

IMAGINE
Apple PAS 10004 - released on 8 october 1971.
Side A:
1) Imagine.
2) Crippled Inside.
3) Jealous Guy.
4) It's So Hard.
5) I Don't Want To Be A Soldier Mama, I Don't Want To Die.
Side B:
6) Gimme Some Truth.
7) Oh My Love.
8) How Do You Sleep?
9) How?
10) Oh Yoko!

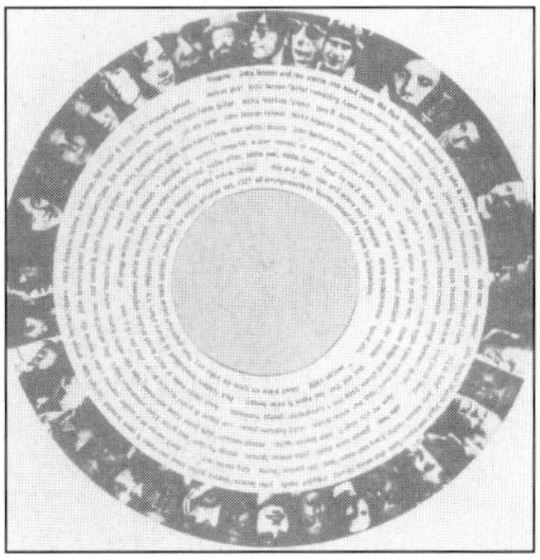

IMAGINE
innersleeve

The LP cover has been designed and made by Yoko. In the film GIVE ME SOME TRUTH, you can see her busy with the design of the cover and discussing it with the designers. The record's first pressings came with a couple of extras, namely a large poster of John sitting behind his white grand piano and a picture post card where John makes a parody on Paul's RAM LP. In stead of holding a sheep by its ears, John holds the ears of a pig. With this picture John makes it clear to Paul that considers him to be a pig. The LP entered the albums chart on 20 October

IMAGINE
Inner sleeve

1971 at number 11 and it rose to number one, where it remained for three weeks. It remained in the Top 10 for 14 weeks. It remained in the charts for a total of 101 weeks. This is the longest period any of John Lennon's LPs remained in the charts in history of the U.K. charts. Whilst the recording was still in the charts, its catalogue number was altered from Apple PAS 10004 to Parlophone PAS 10004. The LP remained available throughout the years and on 17 January 1981 after John had been murdered, it re-entered the LP chart at number 4. This time, it remained in the charts for a total of 10 weeks.
The IMAGINE LP was also John's first LP that reached number one in the British charts.

IMAGINE
Quadraphonic
Germany

List of reissues:
1st reissue:
Parlophone CDP 7 46641 2 - CD
Released on 18 May 1987.
The first release of the IMAGINE album on CD was different as the tracks were edited in a different way. The error was corrected for later releases.

2nd reissue:
Parlophone 5 24858 2 - released on 14 February 2000.
As the old IMAGINE CD sounded rather poor it was decided to use the latest technology to remix the complete LP and to remaster it so that it sounded a lot clearer than ever before. Apart from the CD release, it was also released as a special vynil edition. It came out on 27 March 2000 with the catalogue number Parlophone 5 24858 1.
As well as the sound on the album, the CD booklet and the LP cover were improved. The single LP cover was replaced by a gatefold sleeve. The inner sleeve was printed just like with the original, but the poster and the postcard were missing, the picture with John holding the pig's ears is now depicted on the inside cover.

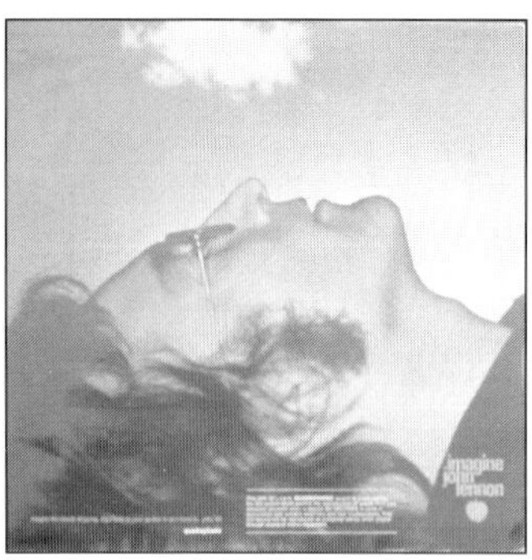

IMAGINE
Quadraphonic
Germany

Quadrophonic version

Apple QPAS 10004.

This version was released in The United Kingdom, Germany, Australia, Japan & The U.S.A. The recordings took place under the supervision of John, George and Phil Spector at the CBS/Sony laboratory. The masters were separated amongst 4 tracks so that the spacey sound that had to come from the 4 speakers would do it credit. The quad mixes show little difference from the stereo ones. As quadrophony did not really get off the ground, it quickly disappeared. Now that we have dolby surround mixes which are used for DVDs and on super CDs, there is a possibility that this record may be reissued at some stage and get a second lease of life.
In 1971, the public were certainly not ready for it, now, thirty years later this system has a better chance to succeed.

IMAGINE
Quadraphonic
Germany

IMAGINE
Reel to reel
USA

JOHN LENNON BOX SET

Apple JLB 8 - released on 15 June 1981.

In order to satisfy the extra demand EMI decided to release a limited box set in 1981 with the eight LPs released between the period from 1970 and 1975. The IMAGINE LP is amongst the 8 LPs. Although the records were identical to the earlier released originals, they came without the extras. The IMAGINE LP though still came with the picture post card and poster; the latter was not exactly the same as in 1971. John's photgraph behind his piano was now shown in double. The lyrics on the inner sleeve were missing, these reissues came with plain white sleeves.
Apart from the eight LPs, a reproduction of the magazine 'The Liverpool Echo's Tribute To John Lennon' was enclosed. The set was a limited edition and therefor did not reach the albums chart.

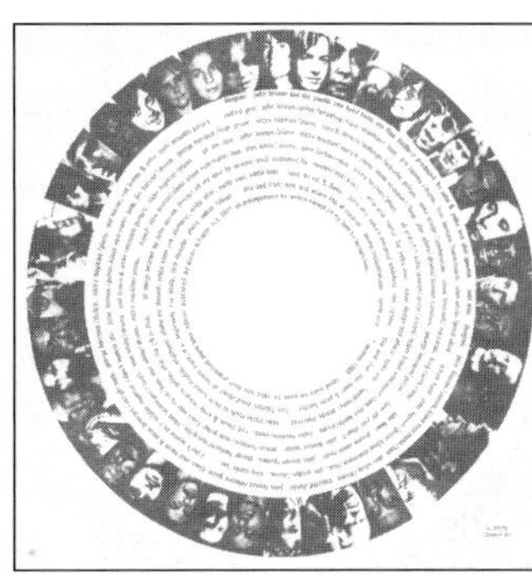

IMAGINE
Inner sleeve-Reel to reel
USA

Singles

Over the years several singles have been released from the IMAGINE LP, especially after John's death.

IMAGINE
Half Speed
USA

Imagine/Working Class Hero

Apple R 6009 - released on 24 October 1975.
Although the single was released all over the world it would take until 1975 until it was finally released on the British market. Notwithstanding its belated release and that "Working Class Hero" did not belong to the IMAGINE sessions but to the JOHN LENNON AND THE PLASTIC ONO BAND, the single became a reasonably big hit.
This single was released to promote the compilation LP SHAVED FISH, which was issued on the same day. I will come back to this later on.
The single entered the singles chart on 4 November 1975 at number 23 and finally reached number 5. It remained in the lists for seven weeks. After John was murdered in the U.S.A., EMI received an enormous amount of advance orders for the "Imagine" single. By 20 December 1980 the amount had run up to 300.000 copies without the record having been announced or promoted .EMI decided to release it quickly and the single entered the singles chart on 3 January 1981 at number 17 and climbed to number one. It remained there for 4 weeks and stayed in the charts for a total of 10 weeks. In 1981, it reached the million mark, meaning that 6 years after its first single release it reached platinum status.

IMAGINE
Half Speed
USA

Love/Give Me Some Truth

Parlophone R6059 - released on 15 November 1982.
To promote THE JOHN LENNON COLLECTION another single was released with a remixed version of "Love" on the A-side and "Give Me Some Truth" on the B-side. The choice of the B-side was unusual as this song can not be found on the compilation album. The single entered the singles chart on 20 November 1982 at number 27. It was not a success and one week later it had disappeared.

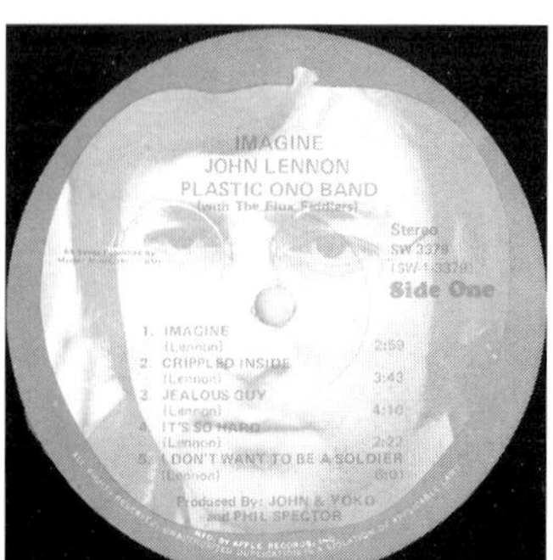

IMAGINE
First release
USA

Jealous Guy/Going Down On Love

Parlophone R 6117 - released on 18 November 1985.

Jealous Guy/Going Down On Love/Oh Yoko!

Parlophone 12R 6117
Released on 18 November 1985.
The 12" and the single appeared on the same day as Paul's single "Spies Like Us".
Also the compilation LP NOW THAT'S WHAT I CALL MUSIC; THE CHRISTMAS COLLECTION (EMI NOX1), including John Lennon's "Happy X-mas (War Is Over) and Paul's song "Wonderful Christmastime" came out on the same day.
The single did not so well, it entered the singles chart on 30 November 1985, reached only number 65 and disappeared again after 2 weeks. Paul's single did better, it entered the singles chart on 21 December 1985 and reached number 13 and remained in the lists for 10 weeks.
The compilation LP with both songs entered the album chart on 30 November 1985 and reached number one; it remained in the lists for 22 weeks.

IMAGINE
8-track
Germany

Imagine/Jealous Guy

Parlophone R 6199 - 7" single
Released on 28 November 1988.

LENNON LP SET
Greece

Imagine/Jealous Guy/Happy X-mas (War Is Over).

Parlophone R 6199 - CD single
Released on 28 November 1988.

Imagine/Jealous Guy/Happy X-mas (War Is Over).

Parlophone 12R 6199 - 12" single -
released on 28 November 1988.
All three releases were issued to promote the IMAGINE-JOHN LENNON film/documentary.
On the same day, EMI also release the first 4 Beatles singles on the akward 3" format, which means that many fans could not play the CDs. Finally, EMI would reissue them on 5" format. Besides the singles, the compilation LP NOW-THE CHRISTMAS COLLECTION, both on vinyl and CD were also released. Both John's "Happy Xmas" and Paul's "Wonderful

LENNON LP SET
UK

IMAGINE
Cassette release
The Netherlands

IMAGINE
South Africa

Cassette release
Indonesia

Christmastime" were amongst the other artists on the vinyl, but John's song was omitted from the CD version. It was the first time that the "Wonderful Christmastime" song appeared on CD.

Imagine/Jealous Guy

Parlophone RP 6199 - 7" picture disc
Released on 5 December 1988.
After the first three releases, a picture disc was also issued. A planned 12" picture disc was cancelled at the last minute.

Imagine/Happy Xmas (War Is Over)/Give Peace A Chance/Imagine (video)

Parlophone LC 0229, 8 88077 0 8 -
Released on 13 December 1999.
The song "Imagine" was often named song of the millenium by various lists, another ideal opportunity to reissue it once again. The CD single version of this release came with a unique extra. For the first time a videoclip was added to a Lennon record. It contained the live recordings of the song from the television programme 'Salute To Sir Lew', which was transmitted on 13 June 1975 which would be the last time John appeared live in front of the public, as a bonus on this 4-track CD. During the broadcast, John performed three songs with the Flux Fiddlers "Slippin' And Slidin'"
(not transmitted), "Stand By Me" and "Imagine". The recordings can only be found on bootlegs. "Slippin' And Slidin" is only in circulation as a recording by a member of the public.

Imagine/Happy Xmas (War Is Over)/Give Peace A Chance.

Parlophone 8 88077 4 6
Released on 13 December 1999.
This time a cassette single rather than a vinyl record.

COMPILATION LPs/CDs

Over the years a number of compilation albums have been released with tracks from IMAGINE. I will only mention the IMAGINE tracks.

SHAVED FISH

Apple PCS 7173
Released on 24 October 1975.
Side B:
1) Imagine.
This is John's first compilation LP, its release date coincided with the release of the "Imagine" single. The LP design was done by Roy Kohara and the drawings, which depicted the hits, by Michael Bryan.
There are a number of errors on the inner sleeve with the lyrics. Phil Spector is mentioned as co-producer for "Cold Turkey", which is incorrect. Spector would only start to work with John as from the following single "Instand Karma".
According to the lyrics, John and Yoko should wish eachother a merry Christmas where in fact they wish Kyoko and Julian a merry Christmas. The review of the LP appeared in the NME of 1 November 1975 written by Charles Shaar Murray. He mentioned the errors in his article and questioned why songs such as "Mother" and "Woman Is The Nigger Of The World" are on this LP whilst they had not been issued as singles. They had actually been singles but had not been released in the U.K. due to the various legal problems surrounding Yoko's songs.
Murray questioned why songs such as "Working Class Heroes", "Don't Worry Kyoko", "How Do You Sleep?" and "Oh Yoko!" were not used in place of the earlier mentioned two songs.
The unexpected happened, Murray received a response and from John. John wrote back that "Cold Turkey" had not been produced by Spector, there was no echo in it, John joked. According to John all the songs on the LP were singles tracks and they would save the song "Don't Worry Kyoko" for a BEST OF YOKO LP. John offered his apologies for the errors with the lyrics and to his defence that he did not have

IMAGINE
Taiwan

IMAGINE
Taiwan

Ultra rare bonus single
Japan

IMAGINE
First release
Japan

IMAGINE
First release
Japan

IMAGINE
First release
Japan

the time to check what EMI was doing as he had to look after his child. Sean was born on 9 October 1975 and was the reason why John turned his back on music for the next five years, concentrating solely on looking after his son. The LP entered the album chart on 11 November 1975 at number 19 and climbed as high as number six. It remained 12 weeks in the lists. After John's murder there was a great demand for the LP again and on 17 January 1981 it re-entered the chart at number 25, rose to number 7 and remained in the lists for eight weeks.
The LP was released on CD for the first time on 26 May 1987 (CDP 7 46642 2). This edition was withdrawn due to the bad sound quality. The CD was reissued on 17 May 1988 with an improved sound quality. The catalogue number and the tracklisting remained the same. The sound was improved by using Sony Solutions No Noise Processing.

THE JOHN LENNON COLLECTION

Parlophone EMTV 37
Released on 8 November 1982.
Side B:
1) Imagine.
2) Jealous Guy.
EMI decided to replace the SHAVED FISH LP with an updated GREATEST HITS LP. It was supported by television advertisement which quickly showed results. Due to this advertising campaign the LP entered the albums chart on 27 November 1982 at number 9, after which it rose to number 1. It remained in the charts for 42 weeks.
During the first few weeks already 300.000 copies and passed the 1 million mark in January 1983, giving it platinum status. EMI had planned to release this LP in 1981, but a difference of opiniion with Geffen over the use of DOUBLE FANTASY tracks delayed its release by over a year. In order to get it released a compromise was made. EMI released it in Europe and Geffen brought out their own compilation for the U.S. market.
EMI released the LP on CD on 23 October 1989 with

the catalogue number EMI EMTV 37. Two tracks were added, although they were not from the IMAGINE LP.

LIVE IN NEW YORK CITY

Parlophone PCS 7301 - vinyl
Released on 24 February 1986.
Parlophone CDP 746192 2 - CD
Released on 24 February 1986.
2) It's So Hard.
8) Imagine.
Fourteen years after the ONE TO ONE concerts the live recordings were released officially on 30 August 1972. Both songs originate from the afternoon show. Apart from vinyl LP and CD, the concert was also released on video. The video also used the afternoon show. The LP entered the albums chart on 8 March 1986 an reached number 55. It only remained in the lists for three weeks.

IMAGINE
Promo flyer
Japan

IMAGINE - JOHN LENNON

Parlophone PCSP 722 - vinyl
Released on 10 October 1988.
Parlophone CD-PCSP 722 - CD
Released on 10 October 1988.
Side C:
1) How?
2) Imagine (rehearsal),
Side D:
1) Jealous Guy.
5) Imagine

IMAGINE
Japan

LENNON

4 CD box, Parlophone CDS 7 95220 2
Released on 29 October 1990.
CD2:
1) Imagine.
2) Crippled Inside.
3) Jealous Guy.
4) It's So Hard.
5) Give Me Some Truth.
6) Oh My Love.

IMAGINE
Japan

IMAGINE
2000 release
UK

7) How Do You Sleep?
8) How?
9) Oh Yoko!

EMI released a beautiful four CD box out with the best of John Lennon. It was to commemorate John's fiftieth birthday.

The IMAGINE LP is well represented on this set. With the exception of "I Don't Want To Be A Soldier Mama (I Don't Want To Die) all the IMAGINE tracks can be found on the second CD. Even after a big promotional campaign, the set did not enter the charts and has since been withdrawn.

LENNON LEGEND

Parlophone 8-21954 1 -Vinyl
Released on 27 October 1997.
Parlophone 8-21954 2 - CD
Released on 27 October 1997.

IMAGINE
2000 release
UK

Side A:

1) Imagine.
4) Jealous Guy,

Once again, they decided to release another double compilation LP/CD. Everything had already been released several times before, so no chart entry for this one.

ANTHOLOGY

Capitol C2 8 30614 2
released on 2 November 1998.

CD1:

ASCOT

IMAGINE
2000 release
UK

9) Imagine - take 1.
11) Baby Please Don't Go.
12) Oh My Love.
13) Jealous Guy.
15) How Do You Sleep?
18) I Don't Want To Be A Soldier, I Don't Want To Die.

Following the tremendous succes of the three ANTHOLOGY CDs by The Beatles, Yoko Ono decided to release her own ANTHOLOGY set of John Lennon. She managed to put together a set every genuine Lennon & Beatles fan was waiting for. The majority of the recordings were new and a welcome addition the large quantity of Lennon outtakes already available through the 'Lost Lennon Tapes' radio shows. In chapter one of this book you can find the background to each number of this set. It was only released on CD. The planned vinyl release has never materilized itself.

IMAGINE
2000 release
UK

WONSAPONATIME

Capitol 4 97639 1 - vinyl
Released on 18 January 1999.
Capitol 4 97639 2 - CD
Released on 2 November 1998.
Side A:
4) How Do You Sleep?
Side B:
1) Imagine.
2) Well (Baby Please Don't Go).
3) Oh My Love.
In order to promote the 4CD ANTHOLOGY set some sort of a BEST OF compilation was made on CD. Strange enough that three months later EMI/Capitol decided to also release a vinyl version. The double LP was only pressed as a limited edition and has now become a sought after item.

IMAGINE
2000 release
UK

IMAGINE
First release
UK

THE UNITED STATES OF AMERICA

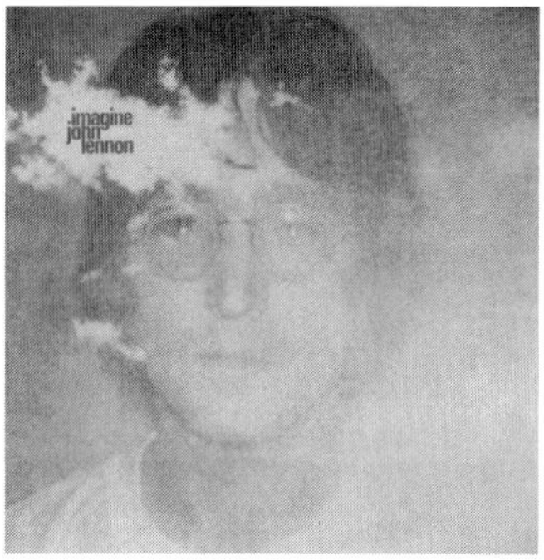

IMAGINE
First CD release

IMAGINE

Apple SW 3379

Released on 7 September 1971.

Side A:

1) Imagine.
2) Crippled Inside.
3) Jealous Guy.
4) It's So Hard.
5) I Don't Want to Be A Soldier Mama, I Don't Want To Die.

Side B:

6) Gimme Some Truth.
7) Oh My Love.
8) How Do You Sleep?
9) How?
10) Oh Yoko!

IMAGINE
First CD release

The LP appeared one month and one day earlier than in Great Britain. Just like in Europe it came with a poster and a postcard. In the U.S. an additional card with John and Yoko was also enclosed. It was possible that you only got one of the card and some LPs had both. The LP entered the hitlists on 18 September 1971 at number 163. It quickly rose to number one where it remained for just one week on 30 October 1971. It remained in the Top 100 for 25 weeks and reached the 1 million dollar mark on 1 October 1971 which gave it gold status. Just like anywhere else the LP was reissued several times on both vinyl and CD.

IMAGINE
First CD release

List of reissues:

Apple:

1st reissue: SW-3379 with print 'MFD BY' - released on 9 September 1971.

2nd reissue: SW-3379 with print "All Rights' - release date unknown.

Capitol:

3rd reissue: purple label with print 'mfd by Apple' - released in 1978.

4th reissue: black rainbow label, without mention Digitally remastered' - released in 1986.

5th reissue: black rainbow label, with notice 'Digitally remastered - released in 1987.
6th reissue: purple label with print 'MANUFACTU-RED' - released in 1988.
6th release: purple label with print 'Manufactured' - released in 1988.

IMAGINE
Second CD release

Special release of IMAGINE.

Mobile Fidelity Sound Lab MFSL 1-153
Released in 1984. White labels this is a special release on high quality vinyl and remastered from the original tapes. An excellent sound quality, unknown for that time. Apart from the vinyl release this version was also released on cassettes with the catalogue number MFSL-C-153.

8 tracks, cassettes, reel to reels and CDs

Apart from vinyl releases, they also released the LPs in various other formats.

IMAGINE
Second CD release

Reel To Reel

Apple/Ampex L-3379- released in 1971.
The reel to reel came in a blue box with a playing speed of 7 1/2 IPS (inches per second). It was only made once and is now very difficult to find.

IMAGINE
Second CD release

8 track:

1st release: Apple 8XW-3379 - released in 1971.
2nd release: Apple 8XW-3379 - released in 1972.
Two editions have been released, the first one came in a white case and the reissue of the following year came with a black case. An 8-track version of the quadrophonic LP was also released in the U.S.A.
It is strange that the vinyl version of the quad LP was not released in the U.S. The American 8-track sounds different than the quad LP released in the U.K., Germany, Australia and Japan.

IMAGINE
First release
Australia

1st release: Apple Q8W-3379 - released in 1971.
2nd release: Apple Q8W-3379 - released in 1974.
The first quad 8-track came in a green case where as the 1974 edition came in a purple one.

Cassettes

1st release: Apple 4XW-3379 - released in 1971.
2nd release: Apple 4XW-3379 - Released in 1972.
3rd release: Capitol 4XW-3379 - released in 1978.
4th release: Capitol 4XW-3379 - released in 1986.
5th release: Capitol/Apple C4-4661
Released in 1991.
The first release came in a white cassette case with paper labels. The second one also came in a white case but with the Apple text printed on the cassette case. The third version is the first Capitol release with the oval logo.
The fourth release comes with an improved sound quality using special XDR techniques.
The fifth version, which is still available toady, come with both the Apple and the Capitol logo on the cassette case and the insert.

IMAGINE
First release
Russia

CD releases
1st release: Capitol CDP-7-46641-2
Released on 10 February 1988.
2nd release: Capitol CDP-7-46641-2
Released in 1988.
3rd release: Capitol/Apple C2-46641
Released in 1991.
4th release: Capitol/Apple C2-46641
Released: 1991 - 1993.
The third release has both the Apple and Capitol logos on the inlay. The third release also has the Apple logo on the CD, where as the fourth release only has the Apple logo on the inlay.

IMAGINE
First release
Russia

IMAGINE (remastered edition)

Capitol CDP-5 24858 2
Released on 11 April 2000.

Just like everywhere else in the world, the remastered CD also appeared in the U.S.A., but no vinyl edition was made.

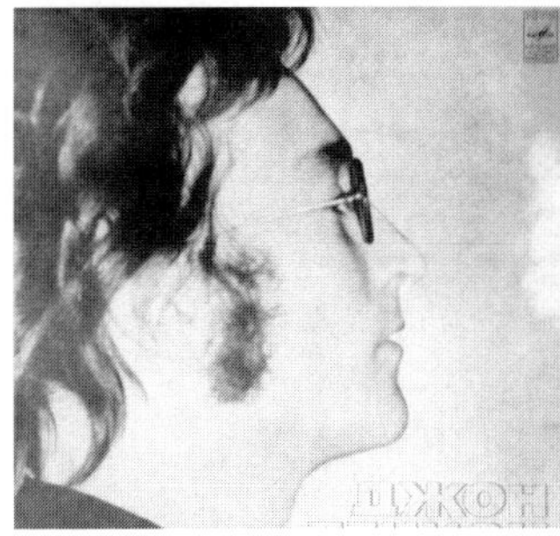

'IMAGINE
Second release
Russia

SINGLES
Imagine/It's So Hard

Apple 1840
Released on 11 October 1971.
Whilst the single was not released in the U.K., Capitol/Apple decided differently and issued it both in the U.S. and all other countries in the world.
The American single, that came without picture sleeve, entered the hit lists on 23 October 1971 at number 20 and would finally reach number 3, where it remained for two weeks. It dropped out of the lists after nine weeks. The single was reissued several times in the U.S.A.:

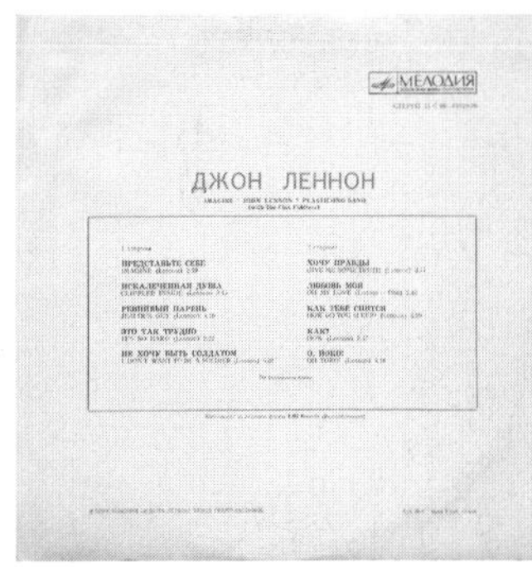

'IMAGINE
Second release
Russia

Apple releases:
1st release: Tan Apple label
Released on 11 October 1971.
2nd release: Apple label with text 'All Rights Reserved' - release date unknown.
Capitol releases:
3rd release: purple label with text 'MFD BY'
Released in 1978.
4th release: black label with coloured rim
Released in 1983.
5th release: purple label with text ' MANUFACTURED' -
Released in 1988.
Capitol/Cema Special Markets release:
6th release: S7-57849
Released in October 1992.

'IMAGINE
Second release
Russia

The first two releases came out pretty well at the same time and the one with the Tan Apple label is the most common one of the two. From the third release onward, the singles were issued on the Capitol label with ever changing colours of the labels.
The most unique pressing is the sixth one, where only 5.000 records were pressed. The first 4.000 were gilt-edged and framed together with the

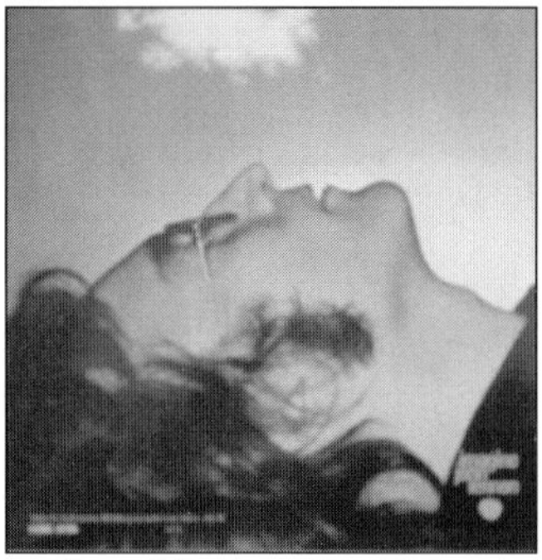

IMAGINE (back)
The Netherlands

"Imagine" lyrics. The remaining 1.000 copies were sold separately. You can still come across the gilt-edged version at Beatles conventions, the copies that were sold separately are very hard to find.

Imagine/Come Together

Capitol SPRO 9585/6

Released in 1986.

This 12" promotional record was made to improve the sales of the SOMETIME IN NEW YORK CITY LP/CD. It came in a plain white sleeve with a sticker.

Jealous Guy/Give Peace A Chance

Capitol B-44230

Released in October 1988.

This single was released to promote the IMAGINE - JOHN LENNON film. There is also a promotional single in circulation with "Jealous Guy" on both sides with the catalogue number Capitol P-B-44230.

IMAGINE
The Netherlands

Retrospective Albums

SHAVED FISH

Apple SW 3421

Released on 24 October 1975.

This album has the same tracklist as its European counterpart. The only difference with Great Britain is that all the tracks from the album have been released as singles in the U.S. The record entered the Billboard charts on 8 November 1975 at number 97 and climbed to number 12, which was its highest position. It dropped out of the lists after 13 weeks.

IMAGINE
Bulgaria

List of releases:
Apple:
1st release: Apple SW-3421
Released on 24 October 1975.
Capitol releases -
All with the catalogue number SW-3421:
2nd release - issued in 1978.
3rd release - also issued in 1978.
4th release- issued in 1983.

5th release - issued in 1983.
6th release - issued in 1989.
The second release comes with a purple label with the text 'MFD By' and the Apple logo is on the rear of the album cover. The third release also has a purple label but this time the Capitol label is on the back of the LP cover. Both the fourth and fifth issued come with the rainbow label, but the fourth release has the Apple logo at the bottom of the back cover where as the fifth release comes with the Capitol logo. The fifth pressing has a purple label again, but this time with the text 'MANUFACTURED'.

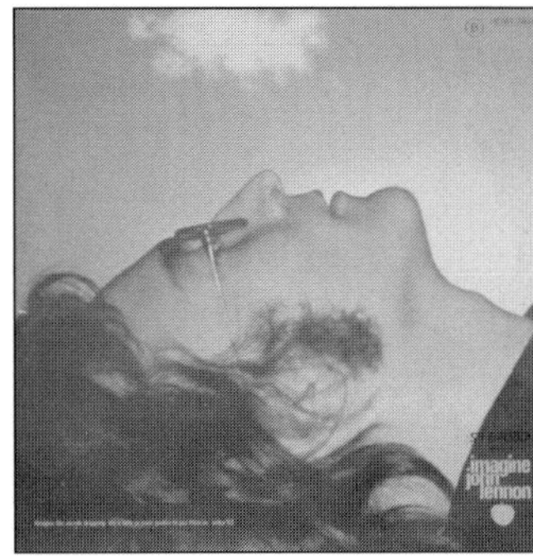

IMAGINE (back)
France

8 track

Apple 8XW-3421 - released in 1975.

Cassettes

Apple release:
4XW-3421 - released in 1975.
Capitol releases
With catalogue number 4XW-3421:
2nd release: issued in 1978.
3rd release: issued in 1986.
Capitol/Apple release:
C4-46642 - released in 1992.
The first release come with an Apple logo and in a black cassette case.
The second release comes in a white case where as the third one comes in a transparent one.
The final version, which is still available today, can be recognized by the joint Apple/Capitol logo on the tape and the inlay.

IMAGINE
first release
France

CDs

All with the catalogue number Capitol/EMI CDP-7-46642-2, unless stated differently:
1st release: issued in 1987.
2nd release: issued in 1987.
3rd release: issued on 17 May 1988.
4th release: issued: 1988-1993.
5th release: Capitol/Apple C2-46642 Issued in 1991.
6th release: Capitol/Apple C2-46642
Issued: 1991-1993.

IMAGINE
Second release
France

IMAGINE
Quadraphonic release
UK

The first version of SHAVED FISH was actually almost immediately withdrawn. It had been pressed in Japan and came with a very poor sound quality. The second one came with a black cover with a small version of the album cover printed on it, the CD was also made in Japan. The fird release comes with the same cover, but the CD was pressed in the U.S. as were all subsequent ones. The fourth release has a cover with the LP cover at its normal size. The fifth release comes with both the Capitol and the Apple logos. The final release was issued in a long box, which were available between 1991 and 1993. Today, the fifth release, without the long box, is still available.

Lost Lennon Tapes
Westwood One release
USA

JOHN LENNON COLLECTION

Geffen GHSP-2023

Released on 3 November 1982.

Side B:

1) Imagine.
2) Jealous Guy.

This retrospectibe LP finally appeared a year later than planned on Parlophone in Europe and on the Geffen label in the U.S.A. The American LP also has a different tracklist as the songs “Happy Xmas (War Is Over)” and “Stand By Me” were omitted. The LP contained 15 songs i.s.o 17. The LP entered the hit lists on 4 December 1982 and reached number 33 as its highest position. It only remained in the lists for six weeks. The various pressings of the LP can be recognized by the stickers which were placed on the album cover. The original had ‘Just Like (Starting Over)’ on the LP cover.The next pressing had a sticker with ‘Woman’, the third one mentioned ‘Watching The Wheels’, the fifth one mentioned ‘I’m Loosing You’.Just to add to the fun a little more, there is also an LP with a sticker ‘Grammy Award Winner’.
A promotional record is also in circulation. The LP is identical to the released version with the difference that ‘Promotion Copy’ is printed in gold letters on the rear of the album cover.

Lost Lennon Tapes
Westwood One release
USA

8 track

Geffen GEF-L8-2023
Released in 1982.

Quadraphonic 8 track
First release
USA

Cassettes

1st release: Geffen L5-2023 - released in 1982.
2nd release: Geffen L5-2023 - released in 1982.
3rd release: Geffen W5-2023 - released in 1982.
4th release: Capitol C4-91516 - released in 1995.
5th release: Capitol/BMG C173627
Released in 1995.
6th release: Capitol/Columbia House 1T1-8287 - released in 1995.
Just like with the vinyl, the first releases were made on the Geffen label.
The first one came in a white cassette case, the second one in a transparent one and the third one was a record club release, also in a white case.
As from the fourth release, the rights returned to Capitol and also released the album in transparent cases. This version is still available today.
The two final releases are record club editions. They can be recognized by the text 'Mfd for BMG' and 'Mfd for Columbia House'. These edition could not be purchased in the record shops.

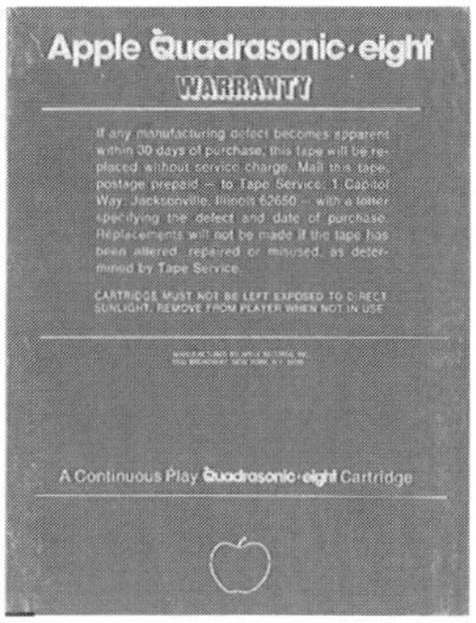

Quadraphonic 8 track
First release
USA

CDs

Catalogue numbers are Capitol C2-91516, unless stated otherwise:
1st release: issued on 29 January 1990.
2nd release:
Issued between 29 January 1990 and 1993.
3rd release:
Issued between 29 January 1990 and 1993.
4th release: Capitol/Columbia House DP-7-591516
Released in 1991.
5th release:
Capitol/BMG D-173627 - released in 1991.
6th release: Capitol/Apple - released in 1991.
The CD contains 4 songs, which are not on the LP. These are "Happy Xmas (War Is Over)", "Stand By Me", "Move Over Ms. L" and "Cold Turkey".

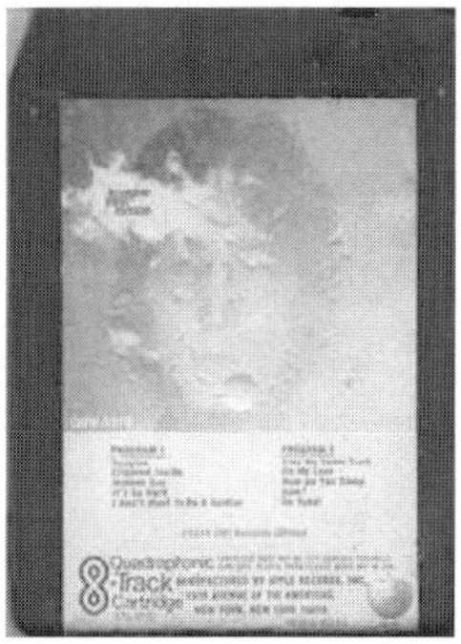

Quadraphonic 8 track
Second release
USA

IMAGINE
Testpressing
Israel

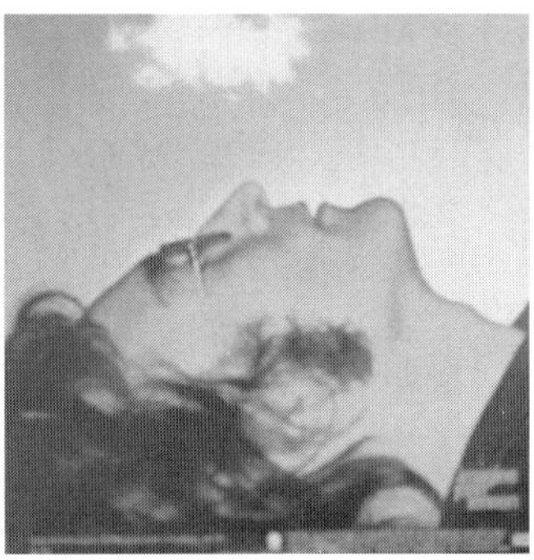

IMAGINE (back)
Canada

IMAGINE
Canada

The first releases were sold separately and the second and third ones came in a long box.
The fourth and fifth releases are record club editions.
The sixth release is still available today and has both Capitol and Apple logo on the CD and the cover.

LIVE IN NEW YORK CITY

The LP was released in the U.S.A. on 21 February 1986. The tracklist was the same as the European version. Three different versions appeared in the U.S.:

1st release: Capitol SV-12451
Released on 21 February 1986.
2nd release: Capitol/Columbia House SV-512451 - Released in 1986.
3rd release: Capitol/RCA SV-12451/R-144497 - Released in 1986.

The first release could be purchased in the shops where as the others were special record club editions. This can be recognized from the printing on the labels and on the album covers. It is mentioned that they were made for Columbia House or for RCA Music Service. As they were not available through the shops, they are now sought after items.

8-track

Capitol S-144497 - released in 1986.
This one-off was made for the RCA record club.

Cassettes

1st and 2nd releases:
Capitol 4XV-12451 - released in 1986.
3rd release: Capitol 4XV-512451
Released: 1986-1987.
4th release: Capitol C-144497
Released: 1986-1987.

The first release comes in a white cassette case with the oval Capitol logo. The second one comes in a transparent case. The third one is a special record club edition for Columbia Records Club and the fourth one for RCA Records Club.

Apart from the usual releases, there are also two different promotional versions of this cassette. The first one comes with a transparent case where as the second one comes in a metal holder.

IMAGINE
Germany

CDs
Catalogue numbers are Capitol CDP-7-46192-2, unless stated otherwise:
1st release: issued on 23 May 1986.
2nd release: issued in 1986.
3rd release: issued in 1987.
4th release: Capitol/RCA D-144497
Released: 1986-87.
5th release: Capitol/BMG D-144497
Issued in 1986.
6th release: Capitol/Columbia House CDP-546196 - Issued in 1986.
The first version appeared both with British and U.S. pressings. The second version came with a sticker saying that it had been made in England.
For the third version the sticker was removed but it was still pressed in England. The CD remained available until 1993. The last three versions are record club editions.

SHAVED FISH
First rerelease
UK

IMAGINE - JOHN LENNON

Capitol C1-90803 - released on 4 October 1988.
Only one vinyl version has been made from this LP, it was issued with a purple Capitol label and logo.

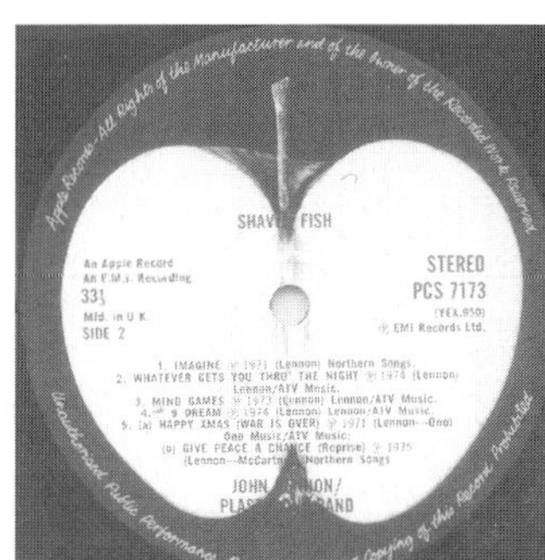

SHAVED FISH
First rerelease
UK

Cassettes

1st release: Capitol C4-90803
Released in October 1988.
2nd release: Capitol/Apple C4-90803
Released in 1992.
Both versions came into circulation for commercial sale in the record shops. The first one did not mention the name Apple/Capitol on the album cover, but the second one did.
The 1992 version is still available today.
There is also a promotional version in circulation,

SHAVED FISH
Israel (detail)

SHAVED FISH
Israel

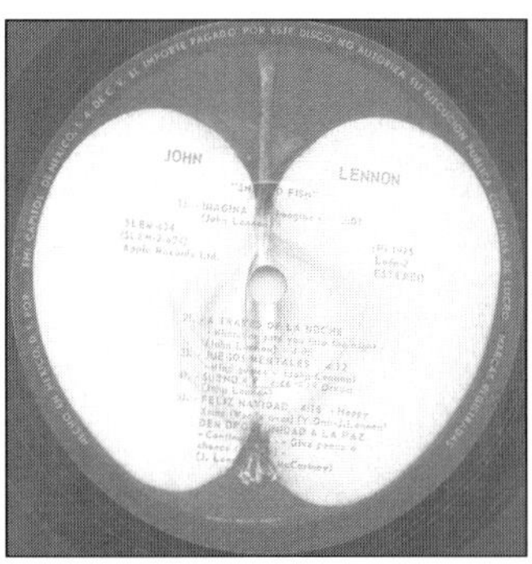

SHAVED FISH
Mexico

which comes with the same tracklist, but promotional copy is printed on both the cassette and the inlay.

CDs

Catalogue number CDP-7-90803, unless stated differently:
1st release: issued on 11 October 1988.
2nd release: issued: 1988-1992.
3rd release: issued: 1992-1993.
4th release: Capitol/BMG 200583
Released in 1988.
5th release: Capitol/Apple C2-90803
Released in 1991.
The first release was sold separately where as releases two and three came in long boxes.
The fourth one is a record club edition.The fifth one comes with both Capitol and Apple logos and this version is still available today.

LENNON BOXED SET

Capitol C4-95220 - released in 1990.
Apart from the CD, Capitol also released it on 4 casssettes, which come with a booklet.

LENNON LEGEND

Capitol 8-21954-1 - released on 10 March 1998.
Whilst the CD had already been issued on 24 February 1998, the vinyl appeared a few weeks later. It came with a sticker with 'special limited edition vinyl release'. It has only been pressed once, comes with an attractive gatefold sleeve and has a purple Capitol label.

Cassette

Parlophone/EMI 8-219 - Geffen L5-2023 - released in 1998. This cassette is still available today.

CDs

Parlophone/EMI 21954-2 - released in 1997.
This CD is still available today.
Other CD releases:
1st, 2nd and 3rd releases: all with catalogue num-

bers Capitol C2-95220, all issued in 1990.
Three versions of this CD are in circulation in the U.S. The first two were pressed in the U.K. On the first version "Imagine" was not mentioned on the box, this was corrected for the second version. The third one was made in the U.S. and can be recognized from the Capitol logo.

SHAVED FISH
India

LENNON ANTHOLOGY

Capitol C28-30614 2 6 -
Released on 3 November 1998.
Just like in Europe, this set only appeared on CD.
A special promotional CD of this set was also made, but I will come back to this.

WONSAPONATIME

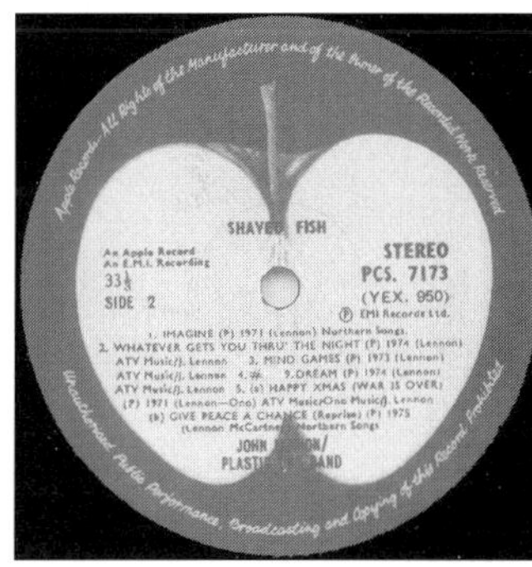

SHAVED FISH
India

CD
Capitol CDP-4 97639 2
Released on 3 November 1998.
Just like in Europe, the so-called 'Best Of ANTHOLOGY' also appeared on CD in the U.S. No vinyl or cassette versions were made.

JAPAN

Not a great deal is known about the Japanese releases. I will mention what I am aware off and additional information is always welcome for future reprints of this book.

SHAVED FISH
Germany

IMAGINE

Apple AP-80370
Released on 25 October 1971.
Side A:
1) Imagine.
2) Crippled Inside.
3) Jealous Guy.
4) It's So Hard.
5) I Don't Want To Be A Soldier Mama, I Don't Want To Die.

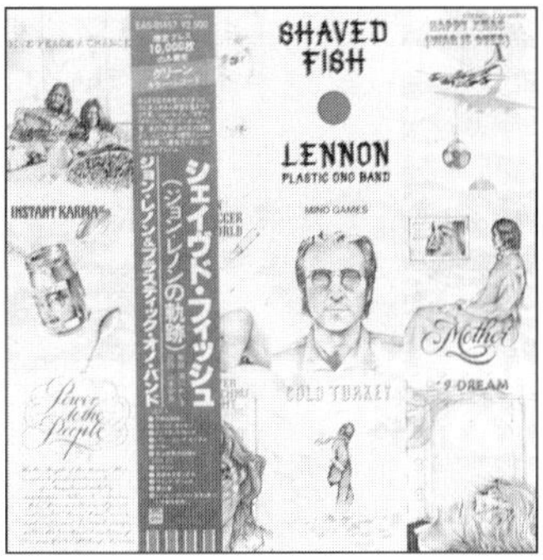

SHAVED FISH
Japan

Side B:
6) Gimme Some Truth.
7) Oh My Love.
8) How Do You Sleep?
9) How?
10) Oh Yoko!
1st release:
Apple AP-80370 - issued on 25 October 1971.
2nd release:
Apple EAZ-80006 - issued on 5 April 1974.
3rd release:
Apple EAS-80705 - issued on 25 January 1984.

The first edition appeared both on red and black vinyl. It is usual in Japan to press the original release on red vinyl.
The first 1.000 copies came with a special promotional single with an interview with John and Yoko in New York, recorded on 2 September 1971.
The second release was only pressed on black vinyl, it concerns the quadrophonic version of the IMAGINE LP. The third release also was pressed on black vinyl only.

SHAVED FISH
Japan

Retrospective LPs

SHAVED FISH

1st release:
Apple EAS-80380 -
Released on 1 December 1975.
2nd release: EMI/Odeon EAS-81457
Released on 15 October 1981.
The first release was pressed on black vinyl whilst the second release was pressed on green vinyl in a very limited edition.

SHAVED FISH
The Netherlands

THE JOHN LENNON BOX SET

1st release: EMI/Odeon EAS-67161-69
Released on 15 June 1981.
2nd release: EMI/Odeon EAS-77019-26
Release date unknown.
The box set was released twice and both pressings

were made on black vinyl. It came with a 20-page booklet with the lyrics, 8 pages of discographies and an edition of the Liverpool Echo
The IMAGINE LP was omitted from the second release for some strange reason!

SHAVED FISH
Uruguay

THE JOHN LENNON COLLECTION

EMI/Odeon EAS-91055 -released in 1982.
The LP has the same tracklisting as the American version.

LIVE IN NEW YORK CITY

Capitol ECS-91160 - released on 1 March 1986.
The record is identical to both European and American versions.

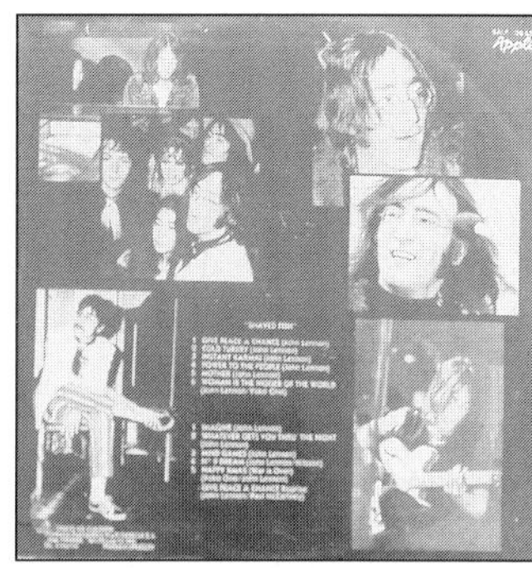

SHAVED FISH
Uruguay

SINGLES

Imagine/It's So Hard

1st release: Apple AR-2929
Released on 10 November 1971.
2nd release: EMI/Odeon EAS-17125
Released in March 1981. Several variants of the first release are in circulation. The first pressing was made on red vinyl and on the Apple label. Repressings were always on black vinyl and on the EMI label. These are always less in value than the original red vinyls. The second release appeared after John's death and were all pressed on black vinyl only.

Imagine/Working Class Hero

Apple EAR-10880 - released on 12 January 1975.
The first "Imagine" single is identical to the American version and all other countries other than the U.K. The second version is identical to the U.K. 1975 version on SHAVED FISH. It was only pressed on black vinyl.

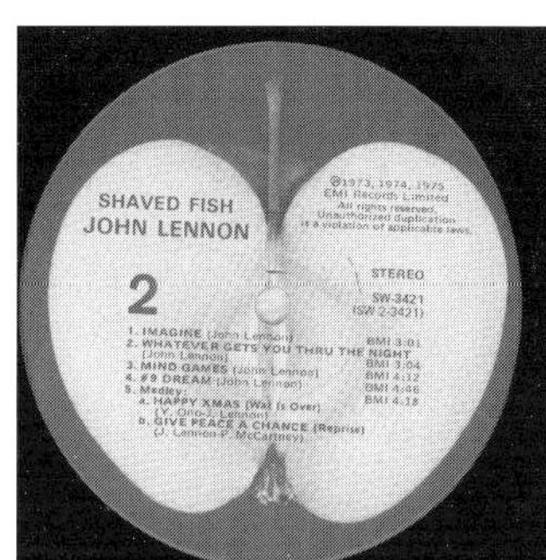

SHAVED FISH
USA

Jealous Guy/Going Down On Love

EMI/Odeon EAS-17133 - released in March 1981.
It was released at the same time as the second version of the original "Imagine" single. It was only pressed on black vinyl.

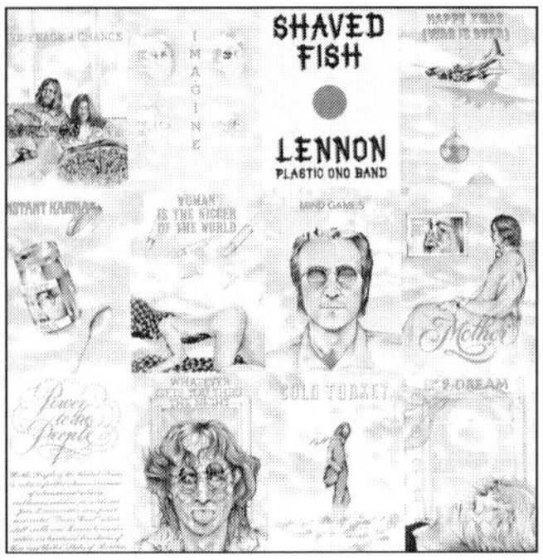

SHAVED FISH
First CD release

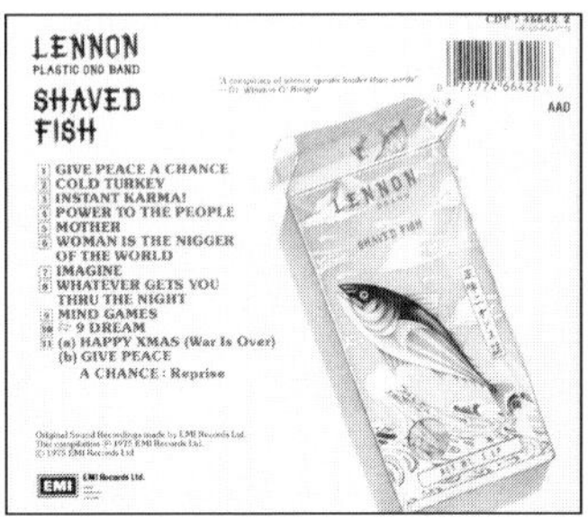

SHAVED FISH
First CD release

SHAVED FISH
First CD release

Love/Give Me Some Truth

EMI/Odeon EAS-17295 - released in 1982.
Released to promote the LENNON COLLECTION LP. It was pressed on black vinyl only.

THE NETHERLANDS

IMAGINE

Apple 5C 062-04914
Released in October 1971.
Side A:
1) Imagine.
2) Crippled Inside.
3) Jealous Guy.
4) It's So Hard.
5) I Don't Want To Be A Soldier Mama, I Don't Want To Die.
Side B:
6) Gimme Some Truth.
7) Oh My Love.
8) How Do You Sleep?
9) How?
10) Oh Yoko!
Radio Veronica tipped the IMAGINE LP to be the LP of the week. It entered the Top 50 on 30 October 1971 and worked its way to number one. It remained in the Top 50 for 21 weeks. After John's death it re-entered the Top 50 on 10 January 1981 and now reached number 12. It remained in the Top 50 for 14 weeks. In Holland, the catalogue numbers were changed a couple of times over the years.

1st release: Apple 5C-062-04914
Released in October 1971.
2nd release: Apple 1A-062-04914
Released during the eighties.
3rd release: Apple 1A-062-04914
Also released during the eighties.
On the 5C release from the seventies, the labels mentioned 'Mfd in the UK' although the vinyl was pressed in The Netherlands. It was also released with the

poster and photograph. For the second release, there is both 'BIEM/Stemra' and 'Mfd in the UK' on the label. Although there is a new catalogue number on the record, the old 5C number can still be found on the album cover. The third release comes in a German LP cover with the catalogue number 1C. The label is the same as the second release.

JOHN LENNON COLLECTION
UK

Retrospective LPs

SHAVED FISH
Apple 5C 062-05987 - released in 1975.
The record entered the Top 50 for the first time on 29 November 1975. It worked its way up to number 28 and only remained in the lists for three weeks.
There was more demand for Lennon LPs after John's death and the album re-entered the Top 50 on 3 January 1981. It now went to number 3 and remained in the Top 50 for seventeen weeks. The LP has been reissued a couple of times over the years.
1st release: 5C-062-05987 - released in 1975.
2nd release: 1A-064-05897
Released in December 1980.
3rd release: 1A-064-05897
Released during the eighties.
The seventies releases can be recognized by the 5C number. The 1A numbers are from after John's death. The second release has either the 1A or the 5C prefix on the LP cover. The third release is a so-called EEC pressing, which means that one country makes the cover and the other presses the vinyl. On the label you can find LC1074 and the label text is both in English and in German.

JOHN LENNON COLLECTION
UK

THE JOHN LENNON COLLECTION

Parlophone 1A-064-78224
Released in November 1982.
This is another EEC pressing, German records in Dutch sleeves. It can be found with both the German and the Dutch catalogue number on the album cover.

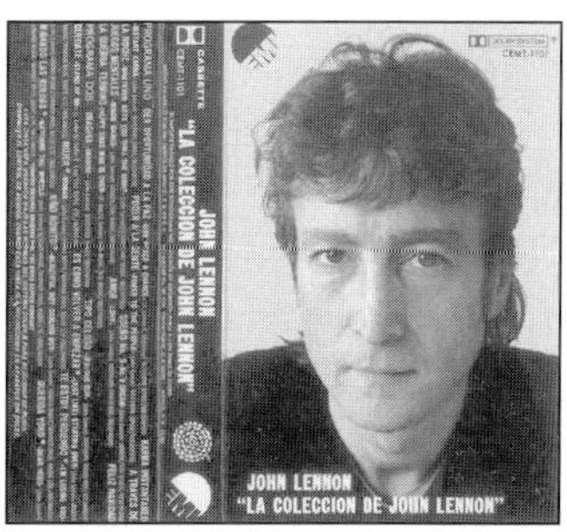

JOHN LENNON COLLECTION
Cassette Tape
Mexico

LIVE IN NEW YORK CITY

Parlophone 1C-064-2404851
Released on 3 October 1986.
No chart entry.
Another German vinyl in a Dutch cover.

IMAGINE - JOHN LENNON

Parlophone 164-7913202
Released on 31 October 1988.
No chart entry.
Again, a Dutch LP cover with a vinyl pressed in Germany.

JOHN LENNON COLLECTION
Promo Album
USA

SINGLES

Imagine/It's So Hard

Apple 5C-006-04940 - released in October 1971.
A substantial amount of label variants are in circulation. If you wish to found out more about this, you can go on the look-out for the book 'Made In Holland Too' by my collegue Ed Dieckmann. It still can be found by another one of my collegues Franck Leenheer, Postbus 11019, 2301 EA Leiden in The Netherlands.
Just like in many other countries, the "Imagine" single has been reissued several time in Holland. It was nominated to be an 'Alarmschijf', which means an alarm disc as it was played every hour by the pirate radio station Veronica.
In Holland, the Top 40 is the best hit list, but there was also a Tip parade. This is some sublist of thirty singles which were tipped to get into the main chart. The record that reached number one in this Tip parade was called the 'alarm disc' of the week. This happened five times to John with "Mother", "Power To The People", "Imagine" (these were three consecutive singles, which all entered the Top 10 of the Top 40 afterwards.), "Happy Xmas (War Is Over)" The latter becoming 'Alarm Disc' twice! This happened first in 1972 and then again in 1981.
Fans could collect the list at their record shop.
The single "Imagine" entered the Top 40 on 6

JOHN LENNON COLLECTION
USA

JOHN LENNON COLLECTION
Germany

November 1971 and climbed to number six. it remained in the Top 40 for ten weeks.
After his death, it was reissued, this time with a picture sleeve, which did not happen in 1971. It also got a new catalogue number. This time it entered the Top 40 on 7 February 1981 and reached number 5. It remained in the lists for eight weeks.

JOHN LENNON COLLECTION
Cassette release
Turkey

List of releases:

1st release: Apple 5C-006-04940
Released in October 1971.
2nd release: Apple 5C-006-04940
Released in 1973.
3rd release: Apple 1C-006-04940
Released during the eighties. The first and third release came without picture sleeve.

Imagine/Jealous Guy/Happy Xmas (War Is Over)

Parlophone 016-2 03089
Released in November 1988 as a vinyl single.
The vinyl was pressed in Germany and the picture sleeve was made in Holland.

JOHN LENNON COLLECTION
CD release

Imagine/Jealous Guy/Happy Xmas (War Is Over)/Give Peace A Chance

EMI CD R6199
Released in November 1988 as a CD single.
The CD single was made in Holland.
The single entered the Top 100 on 7 January 1989, but only reached number 83 and after only three weeks it dropped out of the lists

Imagine/Happy Xmas (War Is Over)/Give Peace A Chance/Imagine (videoclip)

EMI 8 88077 0 - released in 1999.
This CD single, which just like in the U.K., contained the video clip of “Imagine”, entered the Top 100 on 25 December 1999 and reached number 56. It remained in the lists for five weeks.

JOHN LENNON COLLECTION
CD release

SHAVED FISH
Eastern Germany

Jealous Guy/Going Down On Love

1st release: Parlophone 1A-006-07942
Released in June 1981.
2nd release: Parlophone 1A-006-07685
Released in November 1985.
The single was released twice, the first time with a black and white sleeve as a reaction to the cover version by Brian Ferry/Roxy Music. Roxy Music's version was more successful than Lennon's version. Roxy Music's version entered the Top 40 on 21 March 1981 and reached number 7. It remained in the lists for ten weeks. John's single did not enter the charts. In 1985 it was reissued with a picture sleeve and just like in 1981, it did not enter the Top 40.

SHAVED FISH
Second release
The Netherlands

Jealous Guy/Going Down On Love/Oh Yoko!

Parlophone 1AK-060-20 0946 6
Released in November 1985.
Apart from the normal single, they also issued a 12" single with the "Oh Yoko!" bonus track.

Love/Give Me Some Truth

Parlophone 1A-006-07685
Released on 12 November 1982.
Another single that did not manage to enter the hit lists. There are misprinted picture sleeves in circulation where the photograph is not in the middle.

Sheet music

Instand Karma/Oh My Love

EMI 8800497 - released on 29 June 1992 - vinyl.
EMI CDSI 8800492
Released on 29 June 1992 - CD single.
The single was released in The Netherlands as the song had been used as an advert on the television. There was demand for the single and it was released. On 11 July 1992 it entered the Top 40 and reached number 12; it remained in the hit lists for seven weeks. EMI pressed the CD, but allowed Sony to press the vinyl record.

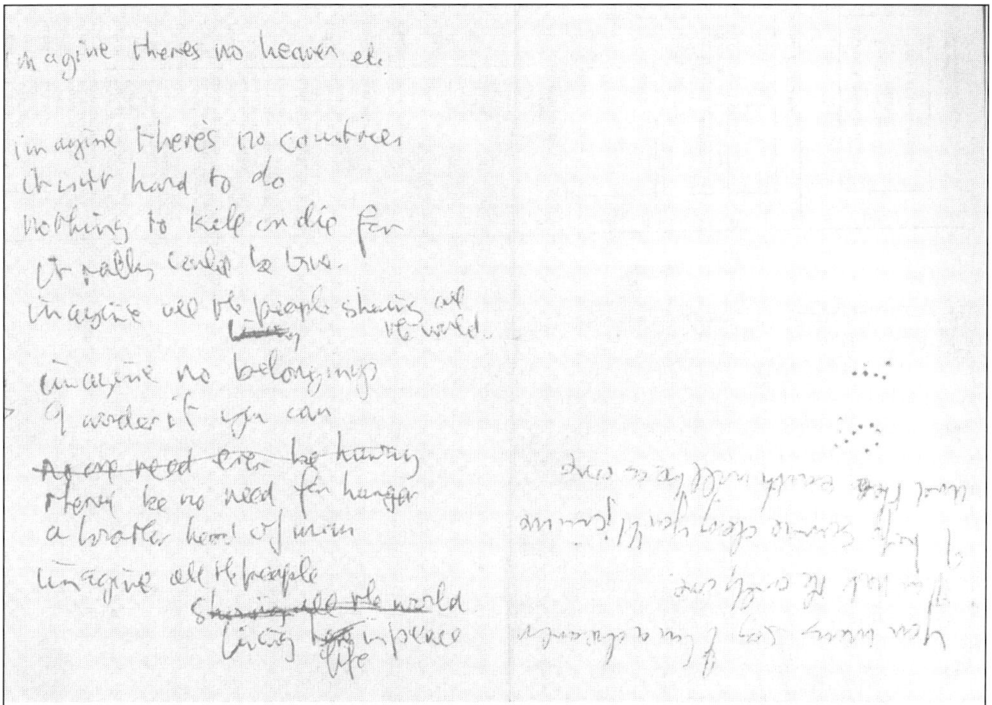

imagine theres no heaven etc

imagine theres no countries
it isnt hard to do
nothing to kill or die for
it really could be true.
imagine all the people sharing all
the world.

imagine no belongings
I wonder if you can
~~And no need even be hungry~~
there'd be no need for hunger
a brother hood of man
imagine all the people
~~sharing all the world~~
living life in peace

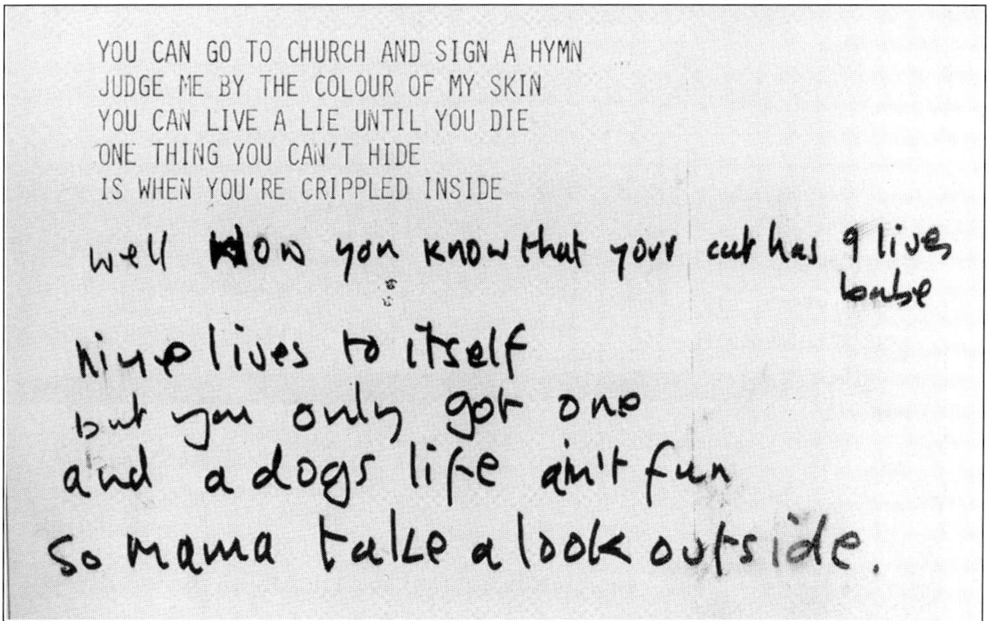

YOU CAN GO TO CHURCH AND SIGN A HYMN
JUDGE ME BY THE COLOUR OF MY SKIN
YOU CAN LIVE A LIE UNTIL YOU DIE
ONE THING YOU CAN'T HIDE
IS WHEN YOU'RE CRIPPLED INSIDE

well now you know that your cat has 9 lives
babe
nine lives to itself
but you only got one
and a dogs life ain't fun
so mama take a look outside.

Text 'Imagine' (3) and 'Cripled Inside'

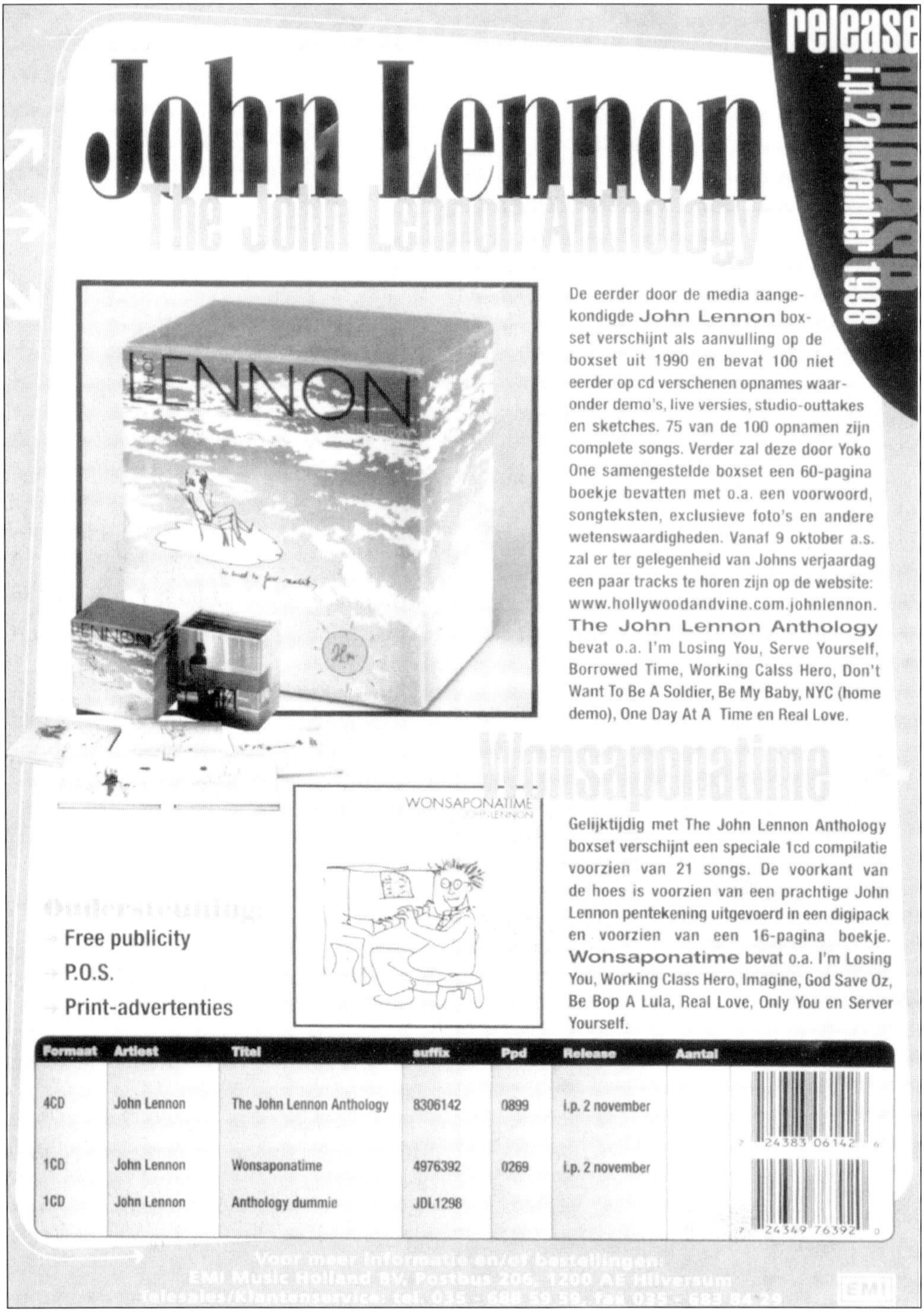

Dutch promotion flyer for record shops

IMAGINE
JOHN LENNON
PLASTIC ONO BAND
PRESENTED TO
JOHN ONO LENNON - WFIL RADIO
TO COMMEMORATE THE SALE OF MORE THAN
ONE MILLION DOLLARS WORTH OF THE
APPLE RECORDS, INC.
LONG PLAYING RECORD ALBUM
"IMAGINE"
CERTIFIED
RIAA
SALES AWARD

ANTHOLOGY
Promo CD

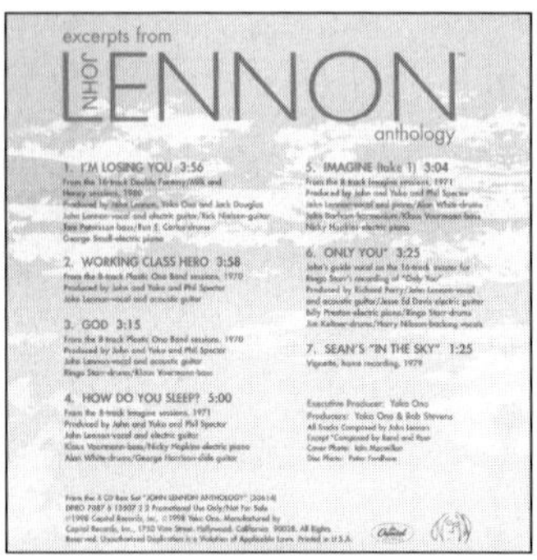

ANTHOLOGY
Promo CD

ANTHOLOGY
Promo CD

RARE AND UNUSUAL RECORDS FROM ALL OVER THE WORLD

Part Two
Acetates And promo's

Apart from commercial records released all over the world, there are also promotional records, acetates, misspresses and strange compilations which have been brought into circulation. Now follows a list of the ones I am aware off.
I am aware that this list is by no means complete.
So, if you have or know about anything else unusual, I look forward to hear from you and it will be included in future reprints.

Acetates

There is an acetate in circulation of the IMAGINE LP and there are others which have been brought into circulation via auctions.
At the Rock 'n' Roll auction by Goodrocking Tonight on 14 and 15 January 1988 an acetate was put up for auction with the following IMAGINE tracks: All My Love, Imagine and Give Me Some Truth.
This 3-track Apple acetate comes with deviating versions.
The song "Oh My Love" in spelled incorrectly as "All My Love".
Apart from the acetate, a test pressing of the IMAGINE LP was also on offer. What is special that this was not an Apple acetate but one from Phil Spector's label.

Imagine - Apple acetate
This one contains a rough mix of the song.

There are misspresses in circulation of the IMAGINE LP where one of the sides plays the music of the RAM LP by Paul McCartney.

In Russia, the records were released on the state owned Melodi label. They records first appeared as flexi singles. Thus, an Imagine EP exists, pressed on very thin blue plastic. It was released on hard vinyl at a later stage.
The EP comes with the following tracks:
JOHN LENNON
Melodia C62-20411 009 - released in 1984.
Side A:
1) Imagine.
2) How?
Side B:
1) Give Me Some Truth.
2) Oh My Love.
Following the EP, they also released the IMAGINE LP in Russia. The first edition came with a strange LP cover, only a photograph with some flowers. When it was reissued, this photograph was moved to the rear of the LP. The photograph was tilted so that the Apple logo can now be seen on its side.
This LPs catalogue number is Melodio 33C 60-08729-30.

100 YEAR EMI
Promo CD

100 YEAR EMI
Promo CD

In Thailand they have released a very strange EP with four different artists and the following numbers:
Side A:
1) Lady Of The Night - Engelbert Humperdinck.
2) Jealous Guy - John Lennon.
Side B:
1) How Can I Tell Her - Lobon.
2) Live And Let Die - Paul McCartney and Wings.
As can be seen, two ex Beatles on one EP. If it is 100% official, I am not so sure, but is certainly a nice item.

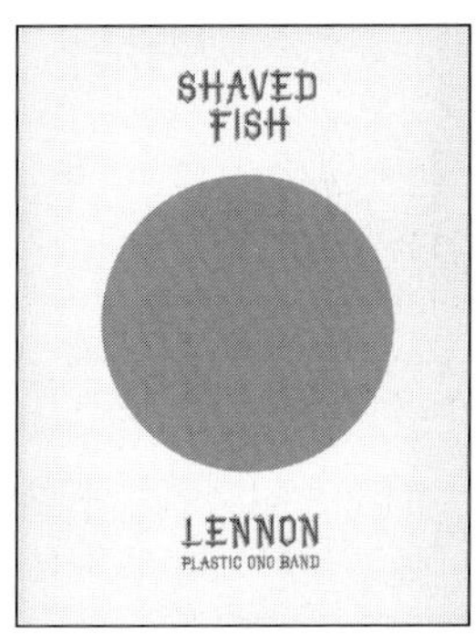

SHAVED FISH
Sheet Music

Imagine postcard
In Poland, the record companies ignored western music and the fans found an answer to this by pressing the music on postcards and send it to eachother. In this book, there is a picture of the "Imagine" single, but I will assume that there are more of the IMAGINE tracks that have been pressed on such postcards.

Promo CD
France

IMAGINE - E.P.
Capitol/EMI EPEM 10616.
Side A:
1) Imagine.
2) It's So Hard.
Side B:
1) Oh My Love.
2) Give Me Some Truth.
This EP from the IMAGINE LP was released in Mexico. The EPs from South America often differed from the ones in Europe and other parts of the world. It came in an attractive picture sleeve.

Promotional records.

Many countries have released promotional records with IMAGINE tracks. I will list the most important ones although there are obviously many more.

Promo CD
France

Vinyl promos

In France a promotional IMAGINE LP has been pressed on blue vinyl.

Disco Promocional Invendavel

EMI 9951 999 -
released in 1986.
Side B:
Come Together - The Beatles.
Imagine - John Lennon.
A promotional compilation LP from Brazil which is very rare with a track by both The Beatles and John Lennon.

Promo CD
France

In 1982, a strange promotional medley by John Lennon was released in Mexico. It has not been released anywhere else. The medleys which can be found on both side, contains the following songs:

LA COLECCION DE JOHN LENNON

EMI SEC-204 - released in 1982.
Playing time side A: 6.38 minutes.
Playing time side B: 6.20 minutes>

There are no IMAGINE songs on the A side, so I will not mention them.

Side B:

1) Imagine.
2) Jealous Guy.
3) Stand By Me.
4) Just Like (Starting Over).
5) Woman.
6) I'm Losing You.
7) Beautiful Boy (Darling Boy).
8) Watching The Wheels.
9) Dear Yoko.

Disco Promocional
Invendavel
Brazil

This promotional record which was made to promote THE JOHN LENNON COLLECTION is now very rare and much sought after item.

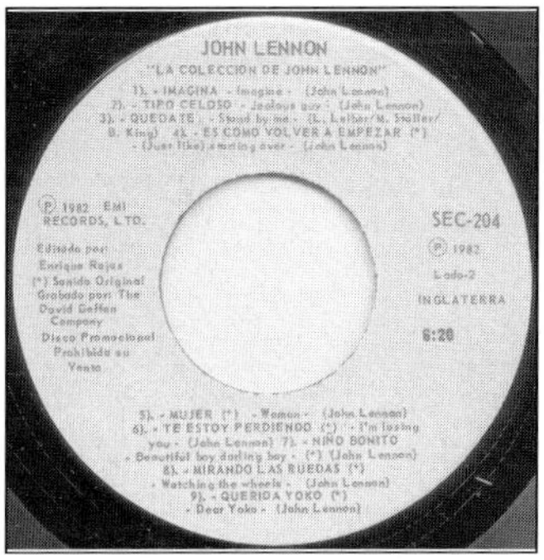

La Coleccion De John Lennon
Promo-Mexico

Promotional CDs

EMI 100-1997. THE FIRST CENTENARY.

EMI CDCNTDJ 1 -released in 1997.
EMI existed 100 years in 1997 and to commemorate this, they issued a special double CD with a look back at their greatest successes. Naturally, The Beatles both as a group and as solo artists are on it.

CD2:

3) She Loves You - The Beatles.
6) Imagine - John Lennon.
11) Mull Of Kintyre - Paul McCartney and Wings.

This set comes in an attractive digipack with a nice booklet.

Promo Flyer
Japan

Jealous Guy

EMI/Capitol DPRO-79417 - released in 1988.
U.S.A. promotional single to promote the film/LP/CD IMAGINE - JOHN LENNON.

ADVANCE LISTENING CD

JOHN LENNON LEGEND
EMI CDPP 037- released in 1997.
A British promotional CD. It comes in a special cover and the print on the CD states

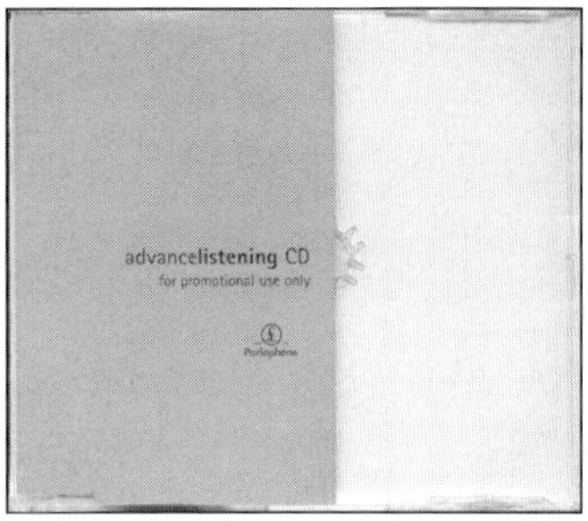

Advance Promo
LEGEND

'Advancelistening CD, for promotional use only'. It has the same tracklisting as the released CD LENNON LEGEND.

Imagine/It's So Hard

EMI 881807 2 -released in 1994.
This is a French 2-track promotional CD to promote the JOHN LENNON COLLECTION.

Excerpts from John Lennon ANTHOLOGY

Capitol DPRO 7087 6 13507 - released in 1998.

1) I'm Losing You.
2) Working Class Hero.
3) God.
4) How Do You Sleep?
5) Imagine - take 1.
6) Only You.
7) Sean's In The Sky.

Two promotional CDs were released to promote the 4CD box LENNON ANTHOLOGY.
The first one is a 2-track promo without IMAGINE tracks.
The second and most common is this 7-track American promo with 2 IMAGINE tracks.

Advance Promo
LEGEND

Imagine/Happy Xmas (War Is Over)/Give Peace A Chance.

Parlophone CDRDJ 6534 - released in 1999.
This is a British 3-track promo to promote the millenium release of the "Imagine" song. It comes with a sticker saying 'Released 13th December'.

Advance Promo
LEGEND

SELECTIONS FROM IMAGINE JOHN LENNON

EMI LENNON 3 \- released in 2000.

1) Imagine.
2) Gimme Some Truth.
3) Jealous Guy.
4) Crippled Inside.

This is a 4-track promotional CD to promote the remastered IMAGINE CD.

JOHN LENNON STARTING OVER

Capitol DPRO 7087 6 15670 2 1- released in 2000. To promote the remixed versions of the three CDs, they released this promotional CD in the U.S.A., it contains, amongst others an interview with Yoko Ono and the IMAGINE songs "Imagine" and "Give Me Some Truth"

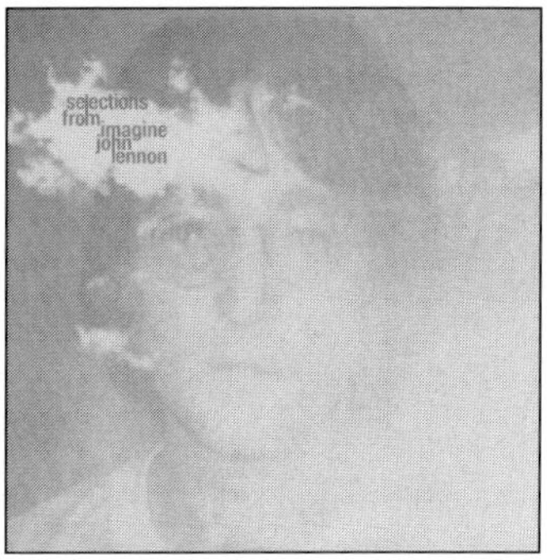

IMAGINE
Selections promo

BOOTLEGS

Apart from the official releases, there are also a great deal of bootlegs been released with IMAGINE outtakes. This certainly happened after the transmissions of the radioshows 'The Lost Lennon Tapes' in the U.S.A. between 18 January 1988 to 23 March 1992 in a total of 215 editions.

All the outtakes which were transmitted have nearly all been released on bootlegs by now. In this review I will first discuss the vinyl releases followed by the CDs, up to the ultimate IMAGINE OUTTAKES sets by Vigotone and Birthday.

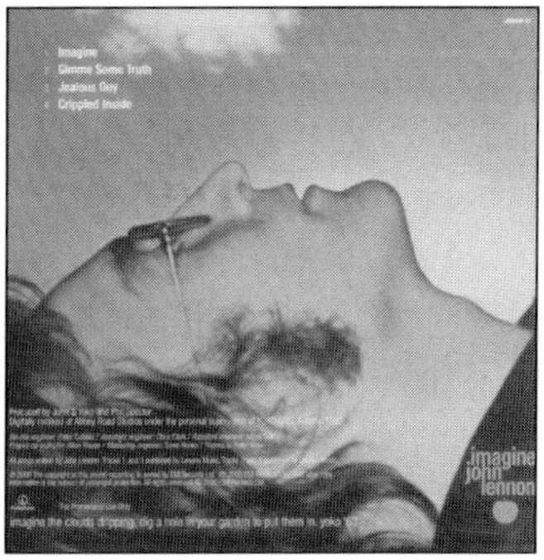

IMAGINE
Selections promo

VINYL BOOTLEGS

IMAGINE LIVE

Over the years, a number of vinyl bootlegs have been released with IMAGINE outtakes which were performed live.

ANGEL BABY

Wizardo 362 - released during the seventies.
Side A:
5) Imagine.
The recording originates from the ONE TO ONE concert from 30 August 1972.

IMAGINE
Selections promo

COME BACK JOHNNY

Melvin MM09- released during the seventies.
Side A:
3) It's So Hard.
Side B:
16) Imagine.
Track 3 is from the ONE TO ONE concert and track

'Imagine' Single CD
Promo
UK

'Imagine' Single CD
Promo
UK

'Imagine' Single CD
Promo
UK

16 from the MIKE DOUGLAS SHOW of 14-18 February 1972.

DAY TRIPPER

CBM 4242 - released during the seventies.
Instand Analysis 1056 - released during the seventies.
King Kong Records - released during the seventies.
Side B:
7) Imagine.
The recordings originate from the JERRY LEWIS TELETON of 6 September 1972.

HOUND DOG

CMB 5040 - released during the seventies.
King Kong 638 - released during the seventies.
Side B:
6) It's So Hard.
ONE TO ONE concert, 30 August 1972.

JOSHUA TREE TAPES

TKWB 1803- released during the seventies.
Side A:
1) Imagine.
Side B:
7) It's So Hard.
"Imagine" is from the ONE TO ONE concert and "It's So Hard" from the MIKE DOUGLAS SHOW.

JOHN LENNON/CHUCK BERRY TELECAST

Catalogue number unknown - released during the seventies.
Side B:
12) Imagine.
From the MIKE DOUGLAS SHOW.

ONE TO ONE CONCERT

CBM - released during the seventies.
Side A:
5) Imagine.
Originates from the ONE TO ONE concerts. It has also been released with the following tittles:
ONE TO ONE CONCERT & ANN ARBOR by King

Kong 641.
ONE TO ONE CONCERT AND MORE by Wizardo 301.
ONE TO ONE CONCERT/MADISON SQUARE GARDEN & ANN ARBOUR.
From the latter, the company and the catalogue number are unknown.

Starting Over
Promo CD

PLOP PLOP ... FIZZ FIZZ

Sean Mark HAR 170- released during the seventies.
Side A:
1) Imagine.
Side B:
8) Imagine.
The first version originates from the ONE TO ONE concert and the second one from the SALUTE TO SIR LEW GRADE television special of 13 June 1975.

Starting Over
Promo CD

TELECAST

CBM 3711- released during the seventies.
TMOQ JL 517 - released during the seventies.
TMOQ 71046 - released during the seventies.
King Kong 642 - released during the seventies.
Side A:
2) It's So Hard.
Side B:
12) Imagine.
These recordings originate from the MIKE DOUGLAS SHOW. It has been reissued several times. It first came with a plain white cover with an insert. Later pressings came with an attractive album cover. Apart from the usual releases, it has also been pressed on a picture disc, this version is very rare.

ANGEL BABY
Vinyl bootleg

TEDDY BOY

JLP 1/2
- released during the eighties.
Side A:
3) It's So Hard.
Side B:
7) Imagine.

BLUES JAM
Vinyl bootleg

Bootleg
Picture Disc
Side A

Bootleg
Picture Disc
Side B

This is a reissue of COME BACK JOHNNY, now with a superb LP cover.

Studio Outtakes/live IMAGINE tracks.

The majority of the takes from the IMAGINE sessions originate from the LOST LENNON TAPES radioshows. Every show has been released officially by Westwood One in a very limited edition, not for commercial purposes, but to distribute amongst the American radio stations. Every show was divided amongst two LP records. The records which all came with the same LP cover were accompanied by a playlist and where the commercials were placed on the records.

There are a total of 214 of these double LPs in circulation, with the exception of the first one, which was a double edition and is divided over 4 LPs, released in a carton box.

The official shows have now become collectors items and are hard to find.

The recordings obviously quickly appeared on bootlegs, first on vinyl and then on CD.

At the start of the shows there were two labels that released the records, there was the BAG label which issued the shows with the title THE LOST LENNON TAPES and they have released a great number of LPs. There also was the PAPERLINE MUSIC label which released a number of LPs with the title ARCHIVES. They only issued 8, all with an attractive LP cover. I will only mention the ones with IMAGINE tracks. After the ARCHIVES I will discuss the BAG releases followed by the CD issues.

ARCHIVES VOL. 2

Paperline Music 8RCH-222

Released during the eighties.

Side A:

I Am The Greatest, takes 1 & 2 - Ascot demo.

Make Love Not War - Ascot demo.

Side B:

How Do You Sleep? - Home demo.

ARCHIVES VOL. 5

Paperline Music 8RCH-555
Released during the eighties.
Side A:
Jealous Guy -Studio demo.

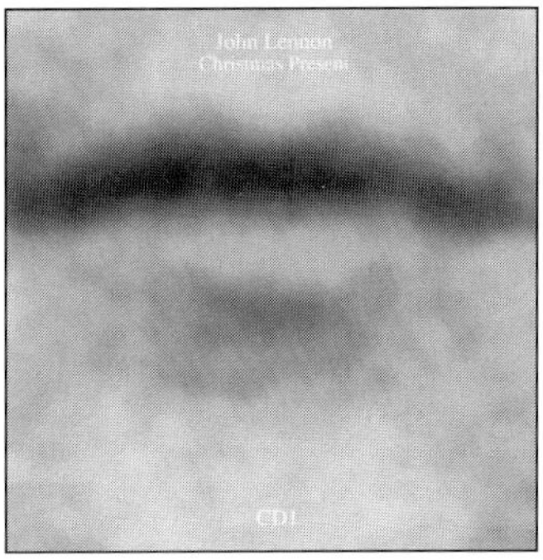

CHRISTMAS
Bootleg CD
Part 1

ARCHIVES VOL. 8

Paperline Music 8RCH-888
Released during the eighties.
Side A:
Crippled Inside - Studio outtake.
Imagine - Outtake.
Side B:
It's So Hard - Outtake.
During the nineties this set was also released on bootleg CD with the same tracklisting as the vinyl edition.

CHRISTMAS
Bootleg CD
Part 2

THE LOST LENNON TAPES VOL. 2

BAG 5074.
Side A:
I'm The Greatest.
Make Love Not War.
How Do You Sleep?

THE LOST LENNON TAPES VOL. 5

BAG 5077.
Side A:
Jealous Guy.

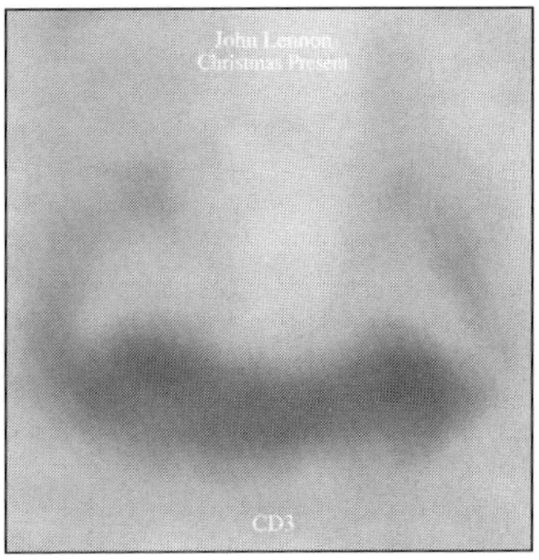

CHRISTMAS
Bootleg CD
Part 3

THE LOST LENNON TAPES VOL. 10

BAG 5082.
Side A:
Imagine.
Crippled Inside.
It's So Hard.

THE LOST LENNON TAPES VOL. 12

BAG 5084.
Side B:
Imagine.

TELECAST
Vinyl Bootleg

THE LOST LENNON TAPES VOL. 13

BAG 5085.
Side A:
Oh Yoko!
How?

THE LOST LENNON TAPES VOL. 14

BAG 5086.
Side A:
Oh Yoko!
Side B:
Give Me Some Truth.
How?
San Francisco Bay Blues.
Oh My Love.
How Do You Sleep?

TELECAST
Vinyl Bootleg

THE LOST LENNON TAPES VOL. 15

BAG 5087
Side A:
I'm The Greatest.
Side B:
I Don' t Want To Be A Soldier.
How Do You Sleep?
Well Baby (Please Don't Go).

THE LOST LENNON TAPES VOL. 17

BAG 5089.
Side B:
Oh My Love
Jealous Guy.

TELECAST
Bootleg
Picture disc

THE LOST LENNON TAPES VOL. 18

BAG 5090.
Side A:
How Do You Sleep?

THE LOST LENNON TAPES VOL. 19

BAG 5091.
Side A:
Oh Yoko!

THE LOST LENNON TAPES VOL. 21

BAG 5093.
Side A:
Oh Yoko!
How?
Side B:
Imagine.
How Do You Sleep?
Oh My Love.
Imagine.

TELECAST
Vinyl Bootleg

THE LOST LENNON TAPES VOL. 24

BAG 5096.
Side A:
Oh My Love (x2).

THE LOST LENNON TAPES VOL. 30

BAG 5102.
Side B:
I'm The Greatest.
How?/Child Of Nature/Jealous Guy.
How Do You Sleep?
It's So Hard.
I Don't Wanna Be A Soldier.

TELECAST
Vinyl Bootleg

THE LOST LENNON TAPES VOL. 33

BAG 5105.
Side A:
Imagine.
How Do You Sleep?
Although the first LOST LENNON TAPES bootlegs were released solely on vinyl LPs, Bag Records also released them on CD from volume 24. Sometimes as single CDs, other times as doubles. The vinyl records appeared on CD as follows:
THE LOST LENNON TAPES VOL. 24 - BAG 5096.
THE LOST LENNON TAPES VOL. 25 - BAG 5097.
THE LOST LENNON TAPES VOL. 26 - BAG 5098.
THE LOST LENNON TAPES VOL. 27 - BAG 5099.
THE LOST LENNON TAPES VOL. 28 - BAG 5100.
THE LOST LENNON TAPES VOL. 29 - BAG 5101.

TELECAST
Vinyl Bootleg

DAYTRIPPER JAM
Vinyl Bootleg

THE LOST LENNON TAPES VOL. 30/31/32 - BAG 5102/3/4 - 2CD.
THE LOST LENNON TAPES VOL. 33/34/35 - BAG 5105/6/7.
Bag Record never released the first 23 records on CD, this was done by the Dutch label Walrus Records.

BOOTLEG CDs with IMAGINE outtakes and live recordings.

Once the vinyl period came to an end, it was to be expected that these recordings would end up on several bootleg CDs. This is exactly what happened. Hundreds of compilation CDs with LOST LENNON TAPES appeared and fans have been buried below them.
I will start with the LOST LENNON TAPES released by the Walrus label.

HOUND DOG
Vinyl Bootleg

THE COMPLETE LOST LENNON TAPES Volume 1 & 2

Walrus Records 002/3- released in 1996.
CD1:
23) I'm The Greatest.
24) Make Love Not War.
25) How Do You Sleep?
CD2:
1) I'm The Greatest.

JOSHUA TREE
Vinyl Bootleg

THE COMPLETE LOST LENNON TAPES Volume 3 & 4

Walrus Records 010/11 - released in 1997.
CD1:
18) Jealous Guy.

THE COMPLETE LOST LENNON TAPES Volume 5 & 6

Walrus Records
014/15 - released in 1997.
CD2:
2) Child Of Nature - Esher demo.

9) Imagine.
10) Crippled Inside.
11) It's So Hard.

THE COMPLETE LOST LENNON TAPES Volume 7 & 8

Walrus Records 017/18- released in 1997.

CD1:
4) How?
25) Imagine.

CD2:
4) Oh Yoko!
19) Oh Yoko!
21) Imagine.
22) Give Me Some Truth.
23) How?
24) San Francisco Bay Blues.
25) Oh My Love.
26) How Do You Sleep?

ONE TO ONE AND MORE
Vinyl Bootleg

THE COMPLETE LOST LENNON TAPES Volume 9 & 10

Walrus Records 019/20 - released in 1997.

CD1:
2) I'm The Greatest.
15) I Don't Want To Be A Soldier.
16) How Do You Sleep?
17) Well (Baby Please Don't Go).

CD2:
15) Oh My Love.
16) Jealous Guy.

TEDDY BOY
Vinyl Bootleg

THE COMPLETE LOST LENNON TAPES Volume 11 & 12

Walrus Records 022/23
- released in 1997.

CD1:
2) How Do You Sleep?
10) Oh Yoko!

CD2:
23) Oh Yoko!
24) How?

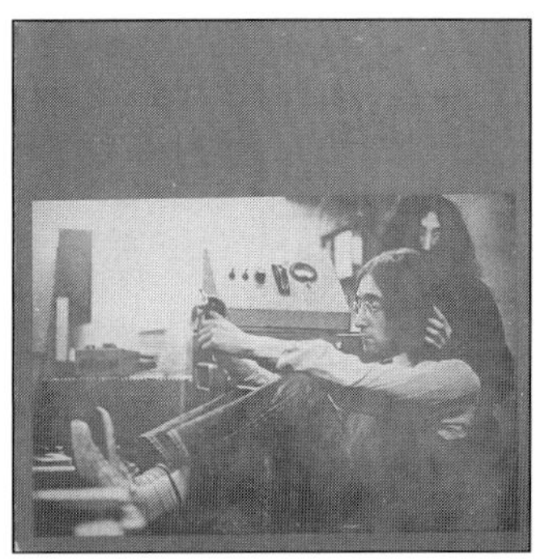

TEDDY BOY
Vinyl Bootleg

ONE TO ONE SHOW
Bootleg CD

25) Imagine.
26) Jam.
27) How Do You Sleep?
28) Oh My Love.

THE COMPLETE LOST LENNON TAPES Volume 13 & 14

Walrus Records 024/25 - released in 1998.
CD1:
1) Imagine.
CD2:
11) Oh My Love.
12) Oh My Love.

ONE TO ONE SHOW
Bootleg CD

THE COMPLETE LOST LENNON TAPES Volume 17 & 18

Walrus Records 028/29
- released in 1998.
CD2:
7) I'm The Greatest.
8) How?/Child Of Nature/Oh Yoko!
9) Oh Yoko!
14) How Do You Sleep?
15) It's So Hard.
16) I Don't Want To Be A Soldier.

THE COMPLETE LOST LENNON TAPES Volume 19 & 20

Walrus Records 030/31- released in 1998.
CD1:
20) Imagine.
21) How Do You Sleep?

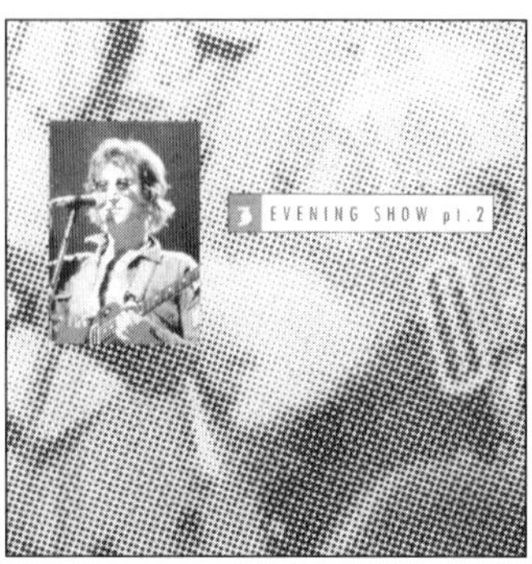

ONE TO ONE SHOW
Bootleg CD

THE COMPLETE LOST LENNON TAPES Volume 21 & 22

Walrus Records 035/36 - released in 1998.
CD1:
10) It's So Hard.
CD2:
30) Crippled Inside.
The recordings of "Crippled Inside" does not originate from the Lost Lennon Tapes, but from a house

party John gave at the start of the seventies.
Once the final vinyl LP was transferred to CD, more playing time was left on the CD and the Walrus label decided to complete it with live recordings. The Mike Douglas shows were placed on CD1 and CD2 contains a number of party recordings of John and his friends.

PLOP PLOP FIZZ FIZZ
Vinyl Bootleg

THE REAL COMPLETE LOST LENNON TAPES

Radio Westwood One
Angry Dog
As I said earlier, a total of 215 shows of the Lost Lennon Tapes have been transmitted.
Both Bag One and Walrus have released highlights from these shows.
In the meantime the CD-r label Angry Dog is busy releasing these shows in full. Fortunately they have had the sense to omit the annoying commercials. The label is still busy releasing them and I will list what they have issued to date

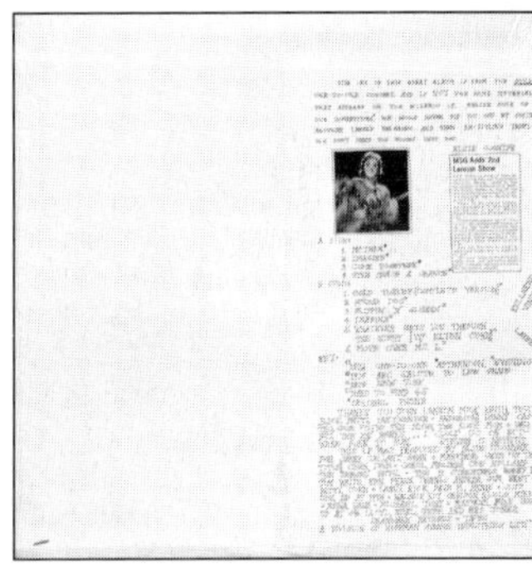

PLOP PLOP FIZZ FIZZ
Vinyl Bootleg

THE REAL COMPLETE LOST LENNON TAPES

Volume 1, January 18, 1988.
Angry Dog AD 2005/6.
CD1:
22) Imagine.
24) How Do You Sleep?/Paulie.
The first show was an introductory one and a double edition. The 4 LPs have been placed on a double CD by Angry Dog. On track 22, John tells us how he had thought about "Imagine" as a children's song as he saw it. Track 24 is about his friendship with Paul and he elaborates about "How Do You Sleep?" which can be heard in the background.

PLOP PLOP FIZZ FIZZ
Vinyl Bootleg

THE REAL COMPLETE LOST LENNON TAPES

Volume 3, February 1st, 1988.
Angry Dog AD 2008.
21) Imagine - live at the Apollo Theatre.

22) About Inspiration Imagine/Outro.
After the live version, John tells us that "Imagine" should have been a Lennon/Ono song, but because of his selfishness at the time, he took all the credits for himself.

REAL COMPLETE
LOST LENNON SHOW
Bootleg CD

THE REAL COMPLETE LOST LENNON TAPES

Volume 7, February 29th, 1988.
Angry Dog AD 2012.
11) Intro 'Child Of Nature'.
12) Child Of Nature.
13) Intro 'Jealous Guy'
14) Jealous Guy.
In this show they talk about the background of "Jealous Guy". We hear a very old version of "Child Of Nature" from the Esher period and then the "Jealous Guy" version.
Unfortunately, John does not talk about this himself.

REAL COMPLETE
LOST LENNON SHOW
Bootleg CD

THE REAL COMPLETE LOST LENNON TAPES

Volume 9, March 14th, 1988.
Angry Dog AD 2014.
3) I'm The Greatest - working demo.
4) I'm The Greatest - studio demo for Ringo.
In this show we can hear John talk about the song he wrote for Ringo.

REAL COMPLETE
LOST LENNON SHOW
Bootleg CD

THE REAL COMPLETE LOST LENNON TAPES

Volume 10, March 21st, 1988.
Angry Dog AD 2016.
6) About the songs J and P wrote 'at' eachother.
7) Too Many People - Paul McCartney.
8) About the songs John and Paul wrote 'at' eachother (cont.).
9) How Do You Sleep? - alternate take .
10) About the songs John and Paul wrote 'at' eachother (cont.). Both John and Paul talk about this controversial song of which we can also hear an alternate version.

Conclusion:
Although the LOST LENNON TAPES CDs and LPs by Walrus and Bag One includes mostly songs, it is also very interesting to be able to listen to the shows as they were
broadcast, complete with the interviews.
It will take a couple of years before they are all available on CD, but this is without any doubt the most important bootleg series in circulation as far as John is concerned.

COMPOSITIONS
Bootleg CD

Live recordings:

Apart from the LOST LENNON TAPES there are also CDs in circulation with live and alternate recordings. I will have a look at the most important ones.

COMPOSITIONS
Bootleg CD

THE ONE TO ONE REHEARSALS VOL. 1

Orange Records Orange Sixteen - released in 1994.
4) It's So Hard.
This double CD had already been released before as a three LP set. They were issued by the same makers as this CD as ONE TO ONE AND ONE IS THREE by Benefit Records.The rehearsals took place at the Filmore East Studios in New York on 26 August .

MISCELLANEOUS TRACKS

Yellow Dog/Orange Records YD-Orange 018
Released in 1995.
1) Imagine.
6) Imagine.
The first version originates from the Jerry Lewis TV show and the second one from the Salute To Sir Lew Grade TV show.

COMPOSITIONS
Bootleg CD

AFTERNOON SHOW (disc one)

Z-904001
- released in 2000.
3) It's So Hard.
13) Imagine.

EVENING SHOW Part 1 (disc two)

Z-904002 released in 2000.

3) It's So Hard.

EVENING SHOW Part 1 (disc three)

Z-904002 - released in 2000.

3) Imagine.

These recordings originate from the ONE TO ONE concerts at Madison Square Gardens on 30 August 1972. The afternoon concert is on disc 1 and the evening concerts is divided between discs 2 and 3.

MISCELLANEOUS TRACKS
Bootleg CD

WARSHIP THE LORD GOD AND SERVE HIM ONLY

MOO-10006.

7) Imagine.

9) Imagine.

12) Imagine.

All three versions originate from the Salute to Sir Lew Grade television show. The first one is a deviating stereo version, the second the actually transmitted version and the third one is a recording in public.

'ONE TO ONE' REHEARSALS
Bootleg CD

JOHN LENNON CHRISTMAS PRESENT

3CD/Cassette set in box with booklet.

WF 001/2/3 - released in 1990.

CD1:

2) Imagine.

11) Jealous Guy.

Track 2 is from the ONE TO ONE concert and track 11 is an alternate take.

CD2:

11) How?

15) How Do You Sleep?

16) Oh My Love.

17) Untitled Jam.

18) Imagine.

Track 11 is an unreleased demo and the other tracks are IMAGINE outtakes.

CD3:

9) Jealous Guy.

10) Imagine.

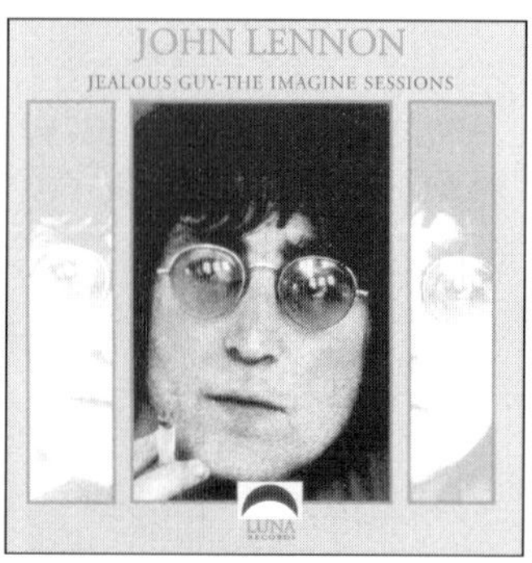

JEALOUS GUY
Bootleg CD

19) Oh Yoko!

Track 9 is an unreleased rough mix, track 10 is from the Mike Douglas Show and final track is an unreleased rough mix as well.

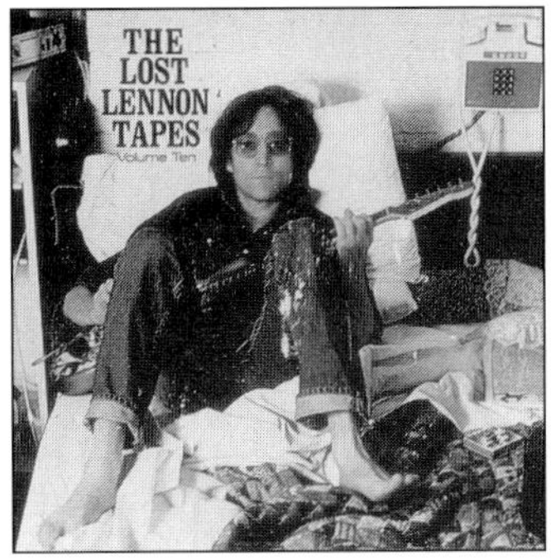

LOST LENNON TAPES
Vinyl Bootleg

COMPOSITIONS

Vigotone VT-191- released in 2000.

1) Make Love Not War.
2) I'm The Greatest.
3) I'm The Greatest.
4) How?
5) Child Of Nature.
6) Child Of Nature.
7) Oh Yoko!
11) Oh Yoko!
12) Oh Yoko!
18) How?
19) How?

In 2000, Vigotone issued a CD with acoustic demos from John. There are a great number of IMAGINE outtakes on this CD in their earlier format. Although these recordings can also be heard during the LOST LENNON TAPES, here we can hear them in a more complete format. This has probably been the tape that was used for the radio show, but we can now enjoy it in full.

IMAGINE-All the outtakes
Vigotone
Bootleg CD set

THIS IS THE TRUTH

BB-CD01 - released in 2001.

Playing time: 79.13 minutes.

3) Crippled Inside.
4-6) Oh Yoko!
7-9) Jealous Guy.
10-12) It's So Hard.
13-15) In Don't Want To Be A Soldier Mama.
16-18) Gimme Some Truth.
19-21) Oh My Love.
22-24) How?
25-27) Imagine.
28-30) Look At Me.

This CD-r contains the 5.1 surround recordings which can be heard on the DVD GIVE ME SOME

IMAGINE-All the outtakes
Vigotone
Bootleg CD set

TRUTH. The sound for the DVD is divided amongst 3 channels and each track is now separated on the CD. The recordings have been reissued by the Birthday label.

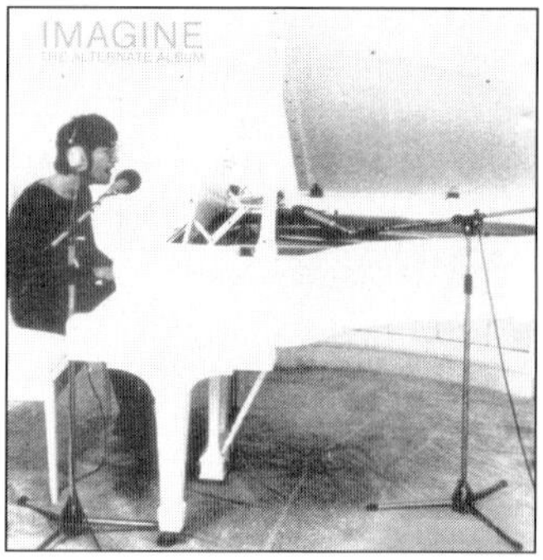

ALTERNATE IMAGINE
Bootleg CD

IMAGINE - QUADROSONICS

Quadraapple-004 - released in 1999.
Playing time: 39.43 minutes.

1) Imagine.
2) Crippled Inside.
3) Jealous Guy.
4) It's So Hard.
5) I Don't Want To Be A Soldier.
6) Give Me Some Truth.
7) Oh My Love.
8) How Do You Sleep?
9) How?
10) Oh Yoko!

The IMAGINE LP had already been released as a quadraphonic LP during the seventies. These version are now difficult to find and when there is a gap, the bootleggers tend to fill it. It has also been reissued by the Birthday label.

IMAGINE-All the outtakes
Vigotone
Bootleg CD set

Alternate IMAGINE CDs

Considering the large quantities of IMAGINE outtakes via the LOST LENNON TAPES, it was obviously only a question of time before CDs would be compiled from these sessions. Although there are many more, I will only review the most important ones.

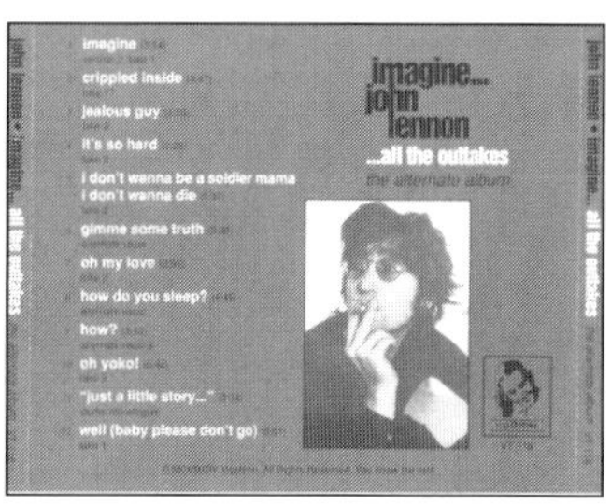

IMAGINE-All the outtakes
Vigotone
Bootleg CD set

IMAGINE - THE ALTERNATE ALBUM

Sidewalk Music SW 89009.
Playing time: 44.23 minutes - released in 1989.

1) Imagine.
2) Crippled Inside.
3) Jealous Guy.
4) It's So Hard.
5) How Do You Sleep?
6) Gimme Some Truth.
7) Oh My Love.

8) How Do You Sleep?
9) How?
10) Oh Yoko!
11) San Francisco Bay Blues.

The first such CD was by Sidewalk which is a Yellow Dog sublabel. It comes with a nice review of the alternate versions that were in circulation. As time progressed this CD would be overtaken by the Vigotone and Birthday releases.

IMAGINE-All the outtakes
Vigotone
Bootleg CD set

JEALOUS GUY - THE IMAGINE SESSIONS

Luna Records LU-9308 - released in 1990.

1) Imagine.
2) Crippled Inside.
3) Jealous Guy.
4) It's So Hard.
5) I Don't Want To Be A Soldier.
6) Give Me Some Truth.
7) Oh Yoko!
8) How Do You Sleep?
9) How?
10) Oh Yoko!
12) How Do You Sleep?
13) Oh My Love.
14) I'm The Greatest.
15) Well Baby (Please Don't Go).
16) How Do You Sleep?
17) Imagine.
20) San Francisco Bay Blues.

IMAGINE-All the outtakes
Vigotone
Bootleg CD set

After the Sidewalk release, the market was flooded with alternates. Luna made a compilation which also included non IMAGINE tracks.

A nice CD, but nothing really new. The CD has already been unavailable for years... better to keep it that way!

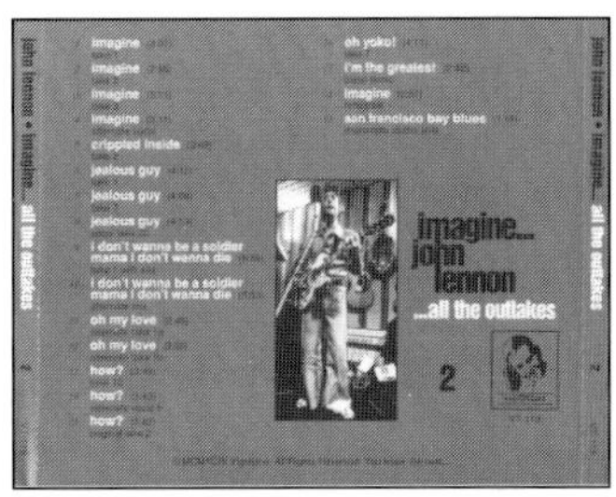

IMAGINE-All the outtakes
Vigotone
Bootleg CD set

IMAGINE - THE SESSIONS

Vigotone VT-CD 08

Released during the nineties.

1) Imagine.
2) Crippled Inside.

IMAGINE-All the outtakes
Vigotone
Bootleg CD set

IMAGINE-All the outtakes
Vigotone
Bootleg CD set

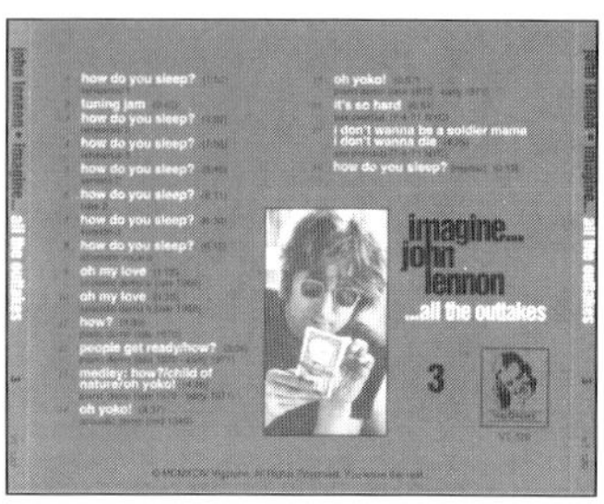

IMAGINE-All the outtakes
Vigotone
Bootleg CD set

3) Jealous Guy.
4) It's So Hard.
5) I Don't Want To Be A Soldier.
6) Give Me Some Truth.
7) Oh My Love.
8) How Do You Sleep?
9) Oh Yoko!
10) Jam - Session outtake.
11) How Do You Sleep? - rehearsal.
12) Oh My Love - version 2.
13) I'm The Greatest - demo.
14) Well Baby (Please Don't Go).
15) How Do You Sleep? - low vocal.
16) Imagine - Piano solo.
17) San Francisco Bay Blues - acoustic solo.

The Vigotone label has released a great deal of John Lennon bootlegs, including this one with IMAGINE outtakes. It was part of a rather unimportant series and would also be overtaken when the label released their 5 CDs.

THE ULTIMATE IMAGINE bootlegs

Following the many compilation CDs, two bootleg labels now came up with the ultimate sets, the American label Vigotone and the Dutch/German Birthday label. Vigotone took the lead, first with a three CD set in a box with a nice booklet and these were copied by the Birthday label.
This was followed by a further double CD by Vigotone and this was also copied by the Birthday label as two separate CDs.
Things now went quiet at Vigotone, the makers were found and the label was void.
Birthday decided to complete the job and produced a further 4 CDs with IMAGINE tracks that were not on the five first ones.
Together, this set of 9 CDs gives a complete review of what is in circulation as far as IMAGINE outtakes.
I will first mention the first five jointly and then the last four by Birthday solely.
Images of both the Vigotone and Birthday releases can be found in this book.

IMAGINE ... ALL THE OUTTAKES VOL. 1

Vigotone VT-118 - released in 1998.

THE IMAGINE OUTTAKES VOL. 1

Birthday Records BR 015 - released in 1998.

Playing time: 48.43 minutes.

1) Imagine - version 2, take 1.
2) Crippled Inside - take 17.
3) Jealous Guy - take 2.
4) It's So Hard - take 2.
5) I Don't Want To Be A Soldier - take 2.
6) Give Me Some Truth - alternate vocal.
7) Oh My Love - take 2.
8) How Do You Sleep? - alternate vocal.
9) How? - alternate vocal.
10) Oh Yoko! - take 9.
11) Just A Little Story - studio monologue.
12) Well Baby (Please Don't Go) - take 1.

IMAGINE-All the outtakes
Vigotone
Bootleg CD set

IMAGINE ... ALL THE OUTTAKES VOL. 2

Vigotone VT-119- released in 1998.

THE IMAGINE OUTTAKES VOL. 2

Birthday Records BR 016- released in 1998.

Playing time: 68.22 minutes.

1) Imagine - take 1.
2) Imagine - take 2.
3) Imagine - take 3.
4) Imagine - alternate vocal.
5) Crippled Inside - take 2.
6) Jealous Guy - take 1.
7) Jealous Guy - take 7.
8) Jealous Guy - vocal take 20.
9) I Don't Want To Be A Soldier - take 1 with sax.
10) I Don't Want To Be A Soldier - alternate mix.
11) Oh My Love - alternate take 1a.
12) Oh My Love - alternate take 1b.
13) How? - alternate vocal b.
14) How? - alternate vocal b.
15) How? - original take 2.
16) Oh Yoko! - take 7.
17) I'm The Greatest - piano demo for Ringo.
18) Imagine - rehearsal.
19) San Francisco Bay Blues

More Sessions
Vigotone
Bootleg CD

More Sessions
Vigotone
Bootleg CD

More Sessions
Vigotone
Bootleg CD

IMAGINE ... ALL THE OUTTAKES VOL. 3

Vigotone VT-120- released in 1998.

THE IMAGINE OUTTAKES VOL. 1

Birthday Records BR 017- released in 1998.
Playing time: 72.22 minutes.

1) How Do You Sleep? - rehearsal 1.
2) Tuning Jam.
3) How Do You Sleep? - rehearsal 2.
4) How Do You Sleep? - rehearsal 3.
5) How Do You Sleep? - version 2.
6) How Do You Sleep? - take 2.
7) How Do You Sleep? - version 3.
8) How Do You Sleep? - alternate vocal b.
9) Oh My Love - acoustic demo - late 1968.
10) Oh My Love - acoustic demo b - late 1968.

More Sessions
Vigotone
Bootleg CD

11) How? - piano demo - late 1970.
12) People Get Ready/How? - piano demo - late 1970/early 1971.
13) Medley: How?/Child Of Nature/Oh Yoko! - piano demo late 1970/early 1971.
14) Oh Yoko! - acoustic demo b - mid 1969.
15) Oh Yoko! - piano demo - late 1970/early 1971.
16) It's So Hard - Sax overdub - 7/4/71 NYC.
17) I Don't Want To Be A Soldier - Sax overdub - 7/4/71 NYC.
18) How Do You Sleep? - reprise.

More Sessions
Vigotone
Bootleg CD

The three CDs were identical. Both labels released the CDs as three separate CDs, Birthday as individual ones where as Vigotone had put them in a luxury box, together with a nice booklet.
In 1999, Vigotone released the follow up, this time a double CD. Birthday decided to copy it, but again as two separate CDs. Birthday's version appeared in 2000.

IMAGINE ... MORE SESSIONS TAPES

Vigotone VT-185/186 - released in 1999.

THE IMAGINE OUTTAKES VOL. 4

Birthday Records BR 070 - released in 2000.

THE IMAGINE OUTTAKES VOL. 5

Birthday Records BR 071 - released in 2000.

Playing time CD1: 57.44 minutes.
Playing time CD2: 61.56 minutes.

CD1:

How Do You Sleep?

1) First rehearsal.
2) Riffing.
3) Another Pass.
4) Tuning Jam.
5) Slow rehearsal.
6) A bit of reggae.
7) 'state 12' low vocal false start.
8) Low vocal false start 2.
9) Low vocal rehearsal.
10) Piano solo false start.
11) Piano solo.
12) Piano solo rehearsal.
13) Eight track take 1.
14) Phil's rhythm instructions.
15) Eight-track take 2.
16) ... From George solo.
17) Imagine.
18) How?
19) I'm The Greatest.

CD2:

It's So Hard

1) John starts tape.
2) King Curtis arrives.
3) Intro playback.
4) John demonstrates on acoustic.
5) King Curtis riffs.
6) First pass and more filling.
7) Second pass.
8) King Curtis asks John a question.
9) Third pass.
10) John gives King Curtis feedback.
11) Another pass at the intro.
12) Another pass at the intro 2.
13) Last Pass.

I Don't Want To Be A Soldier.

14) John discusses the 1966 tour.
15) First playback.

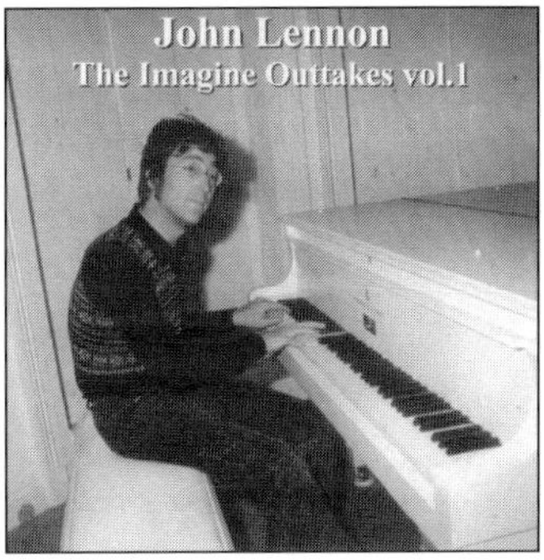

THE IMAGINE OUTTAKES
Vol1
Bootleg CD

THE IMAGINE OUTTAKES
Vol.1
Bootleg CD

THE IMAGINE OUTTAKES
Vol.2
Bootleg CD

THE IMAGINE OUTTAKES
Vol.2
Bootleg CD

16) Playback continued - the first 'hit'.
17) Playback continued - the second 'hit'.
18) John and Curtis talk.
19) First pass.
20) John instructs King Curtis.
21) Second pass.
22) Third pass.
23) Last pass.

The double CD contains the sax overdubs with King Curtis. After this double CD, Birthday Records continues the series.

THE IMAGINE OUTTAKES VOL. 6

Birthday Records BR 087- released in 2001.
Playing time: 72.31 minutes.
Imagine - The film 1972.

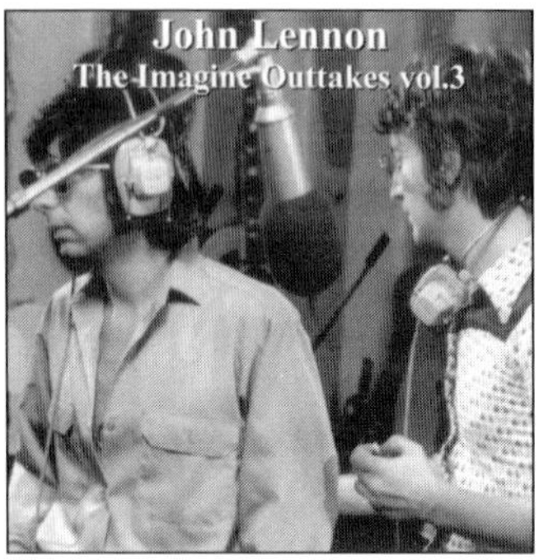

THE IMAGINE OUTTAKES
Vol.3
Bootleg CD

1) Imagine - slower version.
2) Crippled Inside.
3) Jealous Guy.
4) It's So Hard - plus extra guitar part.
5) I Don't Want To Be A Soldier - with John's religious introduction.
6) Give Me Some Truth - with Power To The People intro.
7) Oh My Love.
8) How Do You Sleep?
9) How?
10) Oh Yoko!

Imagine Live

THE IMAGINE OUTTAKES
Vol.3
Bootleg CD

11) Imagine - Apollo Theatre - 17 December 1971.
12) It's So Hard - One To One - 30 August 1972.
13) Imagine - One To One - 30 August 1972.
14) It's So Hard - One To One - 30 August 1972.
15) Imagine - One To One - evening show.
16) Imagine - King Biscuit mix - One to One.
17) It's So Hard - Mike Douglas TV Show - 14 -02-1972.
18) Imagine - Mike Douglas TV Show - 17-02-1972.
19) Imagine - Jerry Lewis TV Show - 6 -09-1972.
20) Imagine - Salute To Sir Lew Grade - 13 -6-75

The CD is divided into two parts, first the IMAGINE - JOHN LENNON film outtakes and then the best live recordings which were in circulation.

THE IMAGINE OUTTAKES VOL. 7

Birthday Records BR 088
- released in 2001.
Playing time: 71.02 minutes.
Imagine Quad
2 channel stereo mix from the direct discrete 4 channel tape, all songs have different mixes.
1) Imagine.
2) Crippled Inside.
3) Jealous Guy.
4) It's So Hard.
5) I Don't Want To Be A Soldier.
6) Give Me Some Truth.
7) Oh My Love.
8) How Do You Sleep?
9) How?
10) Oh Yoko!
Oh My Love Sessions
11) Early run through/studio talk.
12) Rehearsal, complete version.
13) Rehearsal, run through, piano part.
14) George Harrison is tuning his guitar/instrumental run through.
15) Tuning.
16) Rehearsal.
17) Early version with complete intro.
18) John playing piano.
19) Make Love Not War - very early version of Mind Games.
20) Run Through/practising the intro.
21) Instrumental version with intro/practising the intro.
22) Instrumental version with intro/John says fucking hell.

This CD also has two themes, first the quad mixes and finally a great deal of the "Oh My Love" sessions which are in circulation on an unofficial video.

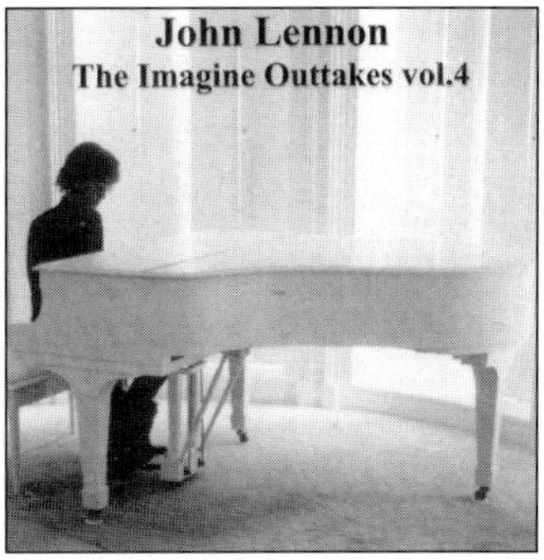

THE IMAGINE OUTTAKES
Vol.4
Bootleg CD

THE IMAGINE OUTTAKES
Vol.4
Bootleg CD

THE IMAGINE OUTTAKES
Vol.5
Bootleg CD

THE IMAGINE OUTTAKES
Vol.5
Bootleg CD

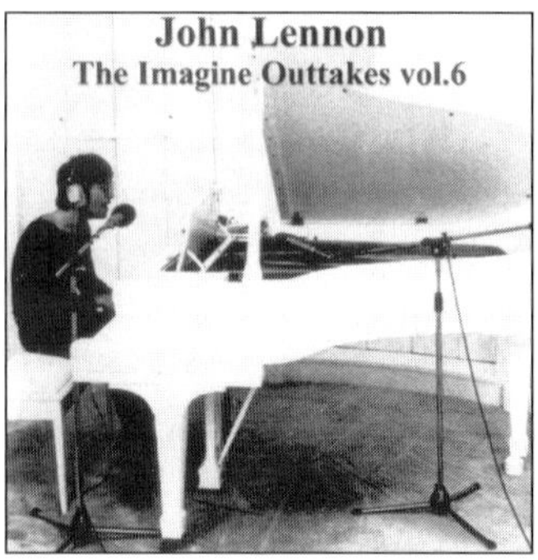

THE IMAGINE OUTTAKES
Vol.6
Bootleg CD

THE IMAGINE OUTTAKES
Vol.6
Bootleg CD

THE IMAGINE OUTTAKES VOL. 8

Birthday Records BR 089- released in 2001.
Playing time: 72.58 minutes.
The Making Of IMAGINE
1) Instrumental.
2) Imagine - piano rehearsal.
3) Imagine - John discussing with Phil Spector.
4) Imagine - different mix used for the making of Imagine film, 2 different parts.
5) Crippled Inside - acapella intro/studio talk.
6) Jealous Guy/studio talk.
7) It's So Hard - short version/studio talk.
8) I Don't Want To Be A Soldier - short version/talk.
9) Give Me Some Truth - recording session.
10) Oh My Love - recording session/studio talk.
11) How Do You Sleep? - recording session.
12) How?
13) Oh Yoko! - session plus studio talk.
14) Look At Me.
5.1 Surround Mixes
Look At Me
15) Centre channel vocals up front.
16) Front channel.
17) Rear channel backing track.
Oh Yoko!
18) Centre channel.
19) Front channels.
20) Rear channels.
The Beatles versions
21) Child Of Nature (=Jealous Guy) - Esher demo.
22) On The Road To Marrakech (=Jealous Guy).
23) Give Me Some Truth - acoustic rehearsal.
24) Give Me Some Truth - rehearsal.
25) Give Me Some Truth - McCartney on vocals.
26) Give Me Some Truth - rehearsal.
All The Rest
27) Crippled Inside.
28) Crippled Inside - live at the house party, early 1970.
29) Imagine - early version from the Imagine movie.
The first 14 tracks of this CD originate from the DVD/video GIVE ME SOME TRUTH.

The 5.1 surround mixes of two of the songs are also on this CD, the remainder are on volume 9.

THE IMAGINE OUTTAKES
Vol.7
Bootleg CD

THE IMAGINE OUTTAKES VOL. 9

Birthday Records BR 090- released in 2001.
Playing time: 65.58 minutes.
The Making of IMAGINE 5.1 surround mixes
Imagine
1) Centre channel.
2) Front channels.
3) Rear channels.
Crippled Inside.
4) Centre channel.
5) Front channels.
6) Rear channels.
Jealous Guy.
7) Centre channel.
8) Front channels.
9) Rear channels.
It's So Hard.
10) Centre channel.
11) Front channels.
12) Rear channels.
I Don't Want To Be A Soldier.
13) Centre channel.
14) Front channels.
15) Rear channels.
Give Me Some Truth.
16) Centre channel.
17) Front channels.
18) Rear channels.
Oh My Love.
19) Centre channel.
20) Front channels.
21) Rear channels.
How?
22) Centre channel.
23) Front channels.
24) Rear channels.

THE IMAGINE OUTTAKES
Vol.7
Bootleg CD

THE IMAGINE OUTTAKES
Vol.8
Bootleg CD

The final CD in this series consists of the remainder of the 5.1 surround mixes. Nine CDs with IMAGI-

NE outtakes and live recordings. Quite a session to listen to them, but a beautiful document about the Making Of ... Imagine! One of best records ever made by John Lennon.

Conclusion:
If you can find this set, you need no longer look out for anything else as far as IMAGINE is concerned. From the many CDs with IMAGINE outtakes, the Vigotone and Birthday releases stand head and shoulders above anything else that is in circulation. DEFINITELY RECOMMENDED!

THE IMAGINE OUTTAKES
Vol.8
Bootleg CD

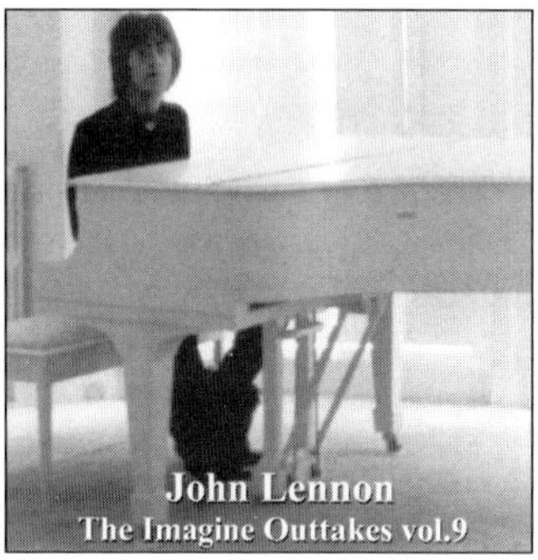

THE IMAGINE OUTTAKES
Vol.9
Bootleg CD

THE IMAGINE OUTTAKES
Vol.9
Bootleg CD

Epilogue

Anthology - The Beatles.
Chronicle - Mark Lewisohn.
Complete Recording Sessions - Mark Lewisohn.
Many Years From Now - Barry Miles.
The Ultimate Recording Guide - Allen J. Wiener.
Records And Memorabilia Price Guide - Perry Cox & Joe Lindsay.
The 910's Guide To The Beatles Outtakes - Doug Sulpy.
The 919's Guide To The Solo Beatles Outtakes - Doug Sulpy & Chip Madinger.
Get Back, the unauthorized Chronicles Of The Let It Be Disaster -
Doug Sulpy & Ray Schweighardt.
The Complete GET BACK SESSIONS- Doug Sulpy
Eight Arms To Hold You - Chip Madinger and Mark Easter.
Black Marked Beatles - Jim Berkenstadt and Belbo.
Not For Sale - Belbo.
The Long And Winding Road - Neville Stannard.
You Can't Do That - Charles Reinhart..
The Beatles After The Break-up - Keith Bathman.
Encyclopedia Of Beatles People - Bill Harry.
The Ultimate Beatles Encyclopedia - Bill Harry.
Record Collector Rare Records Price Guide-
Record Hunter - Tony Rees
The Beatles A Diary - Barry Miles.
Meesterwerken The Beatles 1966-1970 - Azing.
Record Collector Rare Records Price Guide.
Imagine - Andrew Solt and Sam Egan
British Hit Albums - Guinness Publishing
British Hit Singles - Guiness Publishing
Top 40 Hitdossier 8e editie - Johan Slooten
YELLOW DOG, The bootleg collection Vol.2 - Azing Moltmaker
John Lennon Songs - Paul Du Noyer

Magazines:
Beatlesmania - Germany.
Beatles Fan - U.S.A.
Beatles Fan Next Generation.
I would like to express my gratitude to all the writers for their valued information. Apart from these books and magazines, hundreds of hours of music had to be listened to in order to be able to give an objective review about the recordings on these CDs.

The Fan Club

Are you already a member of BEATLES FAN NEXT GENERATION??

Apart from the reference books such as The Album Collection and the Bootleg Collection, Azing also writes the text for the Beatles fan club magazine BEATLES FAN NEXT GENERATION. A magazine that concentrates mainly on the background information about the music of The Beatles. The most recent bootleg releases are reviewed and get a lot of attention in this no nonsense magazine. The periodicals, which will be released at 3 monthly intervals from Autumn 2002, are a magnificent addition to the books written by Azing. Stories that are not in the books such as nice articles about The Beatles' live concerts, news about the group and solo, attractive specials and very detailed reviews about new releases, official and not so official. We write about John, Paul, George and Ringo, not about families and friends, distant acquaintances, this has nothing to do with The Beatles. Music, a lot of music that's what we write about. If you enjoy our books in The Album and Bootleg Collections, you will also enjoy our BEATLES FAN NEXT GENERATION fanzines. They are released in English and our head office is on Merseyside, there could not be a better place for a Beatles fan club magazine. There are currently six back issues which are still available as long as supplies last. They can be ordered from:

BEATLES FAN NEXT GENERATION
63 Whiteside Road,
HAYDOCK
MERSEYSIDE WA11 0JB
ENGLAND
Telephone & Fax 00-44-1744-24511.
E-mail: beatlesfannext@fsmail.net

Annual membership: £20 for the first year and then £15 annually. It can be paid by cheque or postal order, Visa, Mastercard, American Express, Switch, Delta or directly into our bank account Lloyds TSB 30-17-48 1032074 in the name of BEATLES FAN NEXT GENERATION quote membership or visit our website at www.beatlesfannext.com and click on FAN CLUB.

For credit card payments please e-mail us at beatlesfannext@fsmail.net and give your card details, omitting the last four digits for security reasons (there is a 5% surcharge on credit cards and 75p. on debit cards).

Prices are for the U.K., add £2 for Europe and £8 for the U.S.A.

About the writer

About the writer

Azing Moltmaker was born on 28 July 1958 in the Zaan region in North Western Holland and on his fifteenth birthday he received the Beatles single 'Michelle'/'Girl' (Parlophone HHR 139) as a present from his sister when he also got his first record player. Not completely impressed yet he listened to the singles 'Hey Jude' and 'Let It Be' at a school friend's house. The 'Let It Be' single really got him going and he started to collect Beatles records from there onwards. He quickly learned that there are very many different kind of Beatles records and namely the existence of bootlegs was a bottomless source of special recordings. He quickly started to specialise in this sort of records and in 1978 he offered his services to a Beatles Fan Club. By that time Azing had been writing articles about the Beatles and without even having read a single article of his, they rejected him and was told that he did not know enough about The Beatles to write for their magazine. Upset by such arrogance, Azing decided to set up his own fan club; the name of the fan club that was founded on 6 June 1978 was BEATLES FAN RECORDS. The intention was clear from the start, this fan club would be different from all others, the main objective was to discuss the many Beatles records with the accent on the bootlegs. Over the years, the fan club grew and became one of the most flourishing ones, Beatles conventions were organised, even one that lasted for one full week. Records were released, a museum was started and even a touring museum in a converted bus. Unfortunately the bus was stolen and was parked on top of another car by the thieves. Azing was responsible for the costs and the damage and had to sell his Beatles collection. As a result the museum closed, no more fan club magazines were issued and Azing started to do other things. But together with his friend Gerrit Braaksma he always tried to restart the fan club. In the end, it would be his wife Maja Moltmaker who arranged it that a new fan club was set up. The name of this one is BEATLES FAN NEXT GENERATION. A magazine was issued, printed on quality A4 paper and more attractive than anything else that had been done before. A great number of magazines have now already been released, both in Dutch and in English. In 1996, Azing released his first book, MEESTERWERKEN (Masterpieces) The Beatles 1966-1970 in the Dutch language and this book would mark the start of a very long list of books about the music of the Beatles. When our translator Roger Bruneel joined the team it became possible to release the books in English as well. The Album Collection is an English language series and is the largest Beatles series of books in the world; the Dutch language Beatles trilogy added together is the most voluminous Beatles book of all times. With this SGT. PEPPER book, history is made again as never before has such a detailed book about the SGT. PEPPER album been published., Azing is still working at other series of books and apart from The Album Collection, he is also writing a series of books about the various bootleg labels called BOOTLEGS COLLECTION, of which you are now reading one of the first

two volumes. He is also rewriting the MEESTERWERKEN The Beatles 1966-1970 book and this will be reissued as a set of two books. The first book about John Lennon will also be released at the start of 2003. To put it in a nutshell, there is a lot more on its way and that Azing knows a lot about The Beatles has been proven by his books, magazines, , lectures at Universities and what did start as a hobby has now become a full time job!!
Meanwhile, book publishers in The Netherlands have shown interest in Azing's work and from this year, the books in The Album Collection will be released in a Dutch in an adapted and updated version. Discussions are ongoing to release the books in other languages.Due to the numerous releases made and still to come in The Album Collection, The Bootleg Collection and The Solo Collection as well as our Across The Universe books, Azing has become the most productive Beatles book writer anywhere in the world.

Radio shows

Apart from writing his books, Azing also has his own radio show which can be listened to via the Internet. The broadcasts take place at the following times:
Mondays:
Between 7 p.m. and 8 p.m. (CET) Dutch language show 'Here Are The Beatles'
Between 9 p.m. and 10 p.m. English language version of the 'Here Are The Beatles' show.
Between 10 p.m. and 11.30 p.m. Rock Classic Rarities, Beatles and other super bands, with numerous unique recordings.
Wednesdays:
Between 8 p.m. and 11.30 p.m. Rock Classic Rarities.
Thursdays:
Between 9 p.m. and 10.30 p.m. Beatles show.
Between 10. 30 p.m. and 11.30 p.m. Rock Classics Rarities.
The shows can be found on the following address:
www.live365.com/stations/amazingradio 909
It is also possible to communicate with Azing during the transmission via ICQ on number 159325644.

Dutch language books

Foundation Beatles Fan has released a number of books, please find a full list below. The first four have been written in Dutch and have been released in limited editions of 1.000, with hardcover and are numbered individually.

MEESTERWERKEN The Beatles 1966-1970
ISBN 90-803978-1-4.
382 pages - released in 1997.
Retail price directly from us: £15 for hardcover and £10 for paperback

THE BEATLES IN NEDERLAND 1964-1993
ISBN 90-803978-2-2
288 pages - released in 1998.
Retail price directly from us: £17 for hardcover and £10 for paperback

KLASSIEKERS The Beatles 1958-1964
ISBN 90-803978-3-0
640 pages - released in 1998.
Retail price directly from us: £20 for hardcover

WERELDSTERREN The Beatles 1964-1966
ISBN 90-76713-01-4
1000 pages - released in 2000.
Retail price directly from us: £22 for hardcover

SGT. PEPPER'S LONELY HEARTS CLUB BAND
Creatie van een meesterwerk
ISBN ,90-76713-05-7
360 pages-released in 2001
Retail price directly from us: £15 for hardcover

All Dutch language books can be purchased directly from us:

FOUNDATION BEATLES FAN
Bannewaard 24
1824 EC ALKMAAR
THE NETHERLANDS.
Telephone & Fax 00-31-72-5619480.
E-mail: beatlesfan@planet.nl
or by visiting our website www.beatlesfannext.com
If you wish to pay by credit card, please send your card details, omitting the last four digits for security reasons, to beatlesfannext@talk21.com

EXPECTED!!!
MEESTERWERKEN 2A, The Beatles 1966-1968.
MEESTERWERKEN 2B, The Beatles 1969-1970.
The third part of the Dutch trilogy will exist in two parts, the first part which covers the years 1966 to 1968 will be released at the end of 2002 and the second part which covers 1969 and 1970 will appear at the end of 2003. Each book will have approximately 750 pages and will carry on from my last book WERELDSTERREN The Beatles 1964-1966.

ENGLISH LANGUAGE BOOKS

THE BEATLES IN THE NETHERLANDS
1964-1993
ISBN 90-8039-787-3
364 pages - released in 1999.
Retail price directly from us: £20.
Hardcover, numbered limited edition.

LIVERPOOL, HAMBURG AND
THE DECCA TAPES
The Album Collection vol. 0
ISBN 90-803978-4-9
Publishers: Foundation Beatles Fan, Alkmaar, The Netherlands
160 pages - released in 1999.
First edition sold out - reprint due in 2003.

PLEASE PLEASE ME
The Album Collection vol. 1
ISBN 90-803978-5-7
Publishers: Foundation Beatles Fan, Alkmaar, The Netherlands
160 pages - released in 1999.
First edition sold out - reprint due in 2003).

WITH THE BEATLES
The Album Collection vol. 2
ISBN 90-803978-6-5
Publishers: Foundation Beatles Fan, Alkmaar, The Netherlands
160 pages - released in 1999.
Retail price directly from us: £13 - First edition nearly sold out.

A HARD DAY'S NIGHT
The Album Collection vol. 3
ISBN 90-803978-8-1
Publishers: Foundation Beatles Fan, Alkmaar, The Netherlands
160 pages - released in 1999.
Retail price directly from us: £13 - First edition nearly sold out.

BEATLES FOR SALE
The Album Collection vol. 4
ISBN 90-803978-9-X
Publishers: Foundation Beatles Fan, Alkmaar, The Netherlands
160 pages - released in 1999.
Retail price directly from us: £12.

HELP!
The Album Collection vol. 5
ISBN 90-76713-02-2
Publishers: Foundation Beatles Fan, Alkmaar, The Netherlands
224 pages - released in 2000.
Retail price directly from us: £12.

RUBBER SOUL
The Album Collection vol. 6
ISBN 90-76713-03-0
Publishers: Foundation Beatles Fan, Alkmaar, The Netherlands
192 pages - released in 2000.
Retail price directly from us: £12.

REVOLVER
The Album Collection vol. 7
ISBN 90-76713-04-9
Publishers: Foundation Beatles Fan, Alkmaar, The Netherlands
192 pages - released in 2000.
Retail price directly from us: £15 - First edition nearly sold out.

SGT. PEPPER'S LONELY HEARTS CLUB BAND
The Album Collection vol. 8
ISBN 90-76713-06-5
Publishers: Foundation Beatles Fan, Alkmaar, The Netherlands
352 pages - released in 2001.
Retail price directly from us: £15.

MAGICAL MYSTERY TOUR
The Album Collection vol. 9
ISBN 90-76713-07-3
Publishers: Foundation Beatles Fan, Alkmaar, The Netherlands
208 pages - released in 2002.
Retail price directly from us: £15.

ACROSS THE UNIVERSE, Beatles sleeves from around the world, part 1, 1958-1966
ISBN 90-76713-12-X
Publishers: Foundation Beatles Fan, Alkmaar, The Netherlands
288 pages - released in 2002
Retail price directly from us: £20

GET BACK SESSIONS PART 1
The Bootleg Collection vol. 1
ISBN 90-76713-13-8
Publishers: Foundation Beatles Fan, Alkmaar, The Netherlands
152 pages - 32 in colour - released August 2002.
Retail price directly from us: £20

YELLOW DOG
The Bootleg Collection vol. 2
ISBN 90-76713-14-6
Publishers: Foundation Beatles Fan, Alkmaar, The Netherlands
264 pages - 32 in colour - released in August 2002.
Retail price directly from us: £28.

More books are being prepared!!
The Album Collection is a new series of English language books where every Beatles LP gets its own book; all books are released as hardcovers in a numbered limited edition of 5.000 books world-wide; each volume comes with 32 colour pages with unique colour photographs of picture sleeves and album

covers, promotional items, etc... from all over the world.
This series is an absolute must for lovers of the music by The Beatles.
When the series is complete it will consist of 15 or 16 volumes.
Do not take any chances, order your books directly from us:
If you live in The Netherlands or Belgium:

FOUNDATION BEATLES FAN
Bannewaard 24
1824 EC ALKMAAR
THE NETHERLANDS
Telephone & Fax 00.31.72.5619480
E-mail: beatlesfan@planet.nl
or visit our website at www.beatlesfannext.com for further details.
All books cost 20 Euro each, except for SGT. PEPPER which costs 22.50 Euro. Add 7 Euro for postage & package within The Netherlands, from Belgium please contact fan-club for postage costs. Payments can be made via post bank number 44.66.401 or bank number 89.52.36.613 in favour of Stichting Beatles Fan, Bannewaard 24, 1824 EC Alkmaar, with the quotation which book you require.
For Belgium, payment can be made at Generale Bank number 230.0568834.46 in favour of Stichting Beatles Fan, Alkmaar, The Netherlands.
If you wish to pay with Visa or Mastercard, please e-mail your credit card details, omitting the last four digits for security reasons, to beatlesfannext@talk21.com

If you live anywhere else other than The Netherlands or Belgium, please contact:

BEATLES FAN NEXT GENERATION
63 Whiteside Road
HAYDOCK
MERSEYSIDE WA11 0JB
ENGLAND
Telephone & Fax 00.44.1744.24511
E-mail: beatlesfannext@talk21.com
or visit our website at www.beatlesfannext.com for further details

EXPECTED IN MARCH 2003:
THE BEATLES (THE WHITE ALBUM)
The Album Collection Volume 10.

EXPECTED IN MAY 2003:
YELLOW SUBMARINE
The Album Collection Volume 11.

EXPECTED IN AUGUST 2003:
THE BOOTLEG COLLECTION VOL. 3
The Beatles At The BEEB
THE BOOTLEG COLLECTION VOL. 4
Famous labels Vol. 2 - TRADE MARK OF QUALITY

EXPECTED LATER - DATES WILL BE ANNOUNCED WHEN KNOWN:
THE BOOTLEG COLLECTION VOL. 5
GET BACK SESSIONS Part 2

THE BOOTLEG COLLECTION VOL. 6
Famous labels part 3 - VIGOTONE

THE BOOTLEG COLLECTION VOL. 7
LIVE SHOWS

THE BOOTLEG COLLECTION VOL. 8
GET BACK SESSIONS Part 3

Do not miss a single volume from this series!!! Reserve your copy immediately and directly from us. If you purchase the first two volumes, you will be able to keep your limited edition throughout the series!! If you already have a personal limited edition number from the Album Collection, your Bootleg Collection books will come with the same number if you are subscribing to the series. If you have signed a credit card authorisation form, please ask for an updated one, including Bootleg and Solo Collections as well as Across The Universe.
Volume 8 is not the final volume in the Bootleg Collection, more books are being prepared, watch this space.....

EXPECTED ... EXPECTED ... EXPECTED ...

LET IT BE
The Album Collection Volume 12
Publishers: Foundation Beatles Fan, Alkmaar, The Netherlands
Retail price directly from us: £13.
ABBEY ROAD
The Album Collection Volume 13

Publishers: Foundation Beatles Fan, Alkmaar, The Netherlands
Retail price directly from us: £13.

PAST MASTERS
The Album Collection Vol. 14
Publishers: Foundation Beatles Fan, Alkmaar, The Netherlands
Retail price directly from us: £13.

RARITIES
The Album Collection Vol. 15
The concluding volume of the Album Collection, after the series continues with the Solo Collection.
Publishers: Foundation Beatles Fan, Alkmaar, The Netherlands
Retail price directly from us: £13.

PAUL McCARTNEY IN THE NETHERLANDS 1972-1993
The ultimate report about the concerts and television appearance by Paul in Holland, never before published photographs, his vinyl discography, including picture sleeves, LP covers, labels, bootlegs. Another reference book for every Macca fan!!

WHILE MY GUITAR GENTLY WEEPS
The music of George Harrison
The Solo Collection - vol. 2.

The Making of ... BAND ON THE RUN
The Solo Collection - vol. 3.

WHITE ALBUM
The Album Collection vol. 10
AZING

YELLOW SUBMARINE
The Album Collection vol. 11
The Beatles
Yellow Submarine
AZING

LET IT BE
The Album Collection vol. 12
LET IT BE
AZING

ABBEY ROAD
The Album Collection vol. 13
AZING

WHITE ALBUM
The Album Collection vol. 10
AZING

BEATLES AT THE BEEB
The Bootleg Collection vol. 3
THE BEATLES
AT THE BEEB
AZING

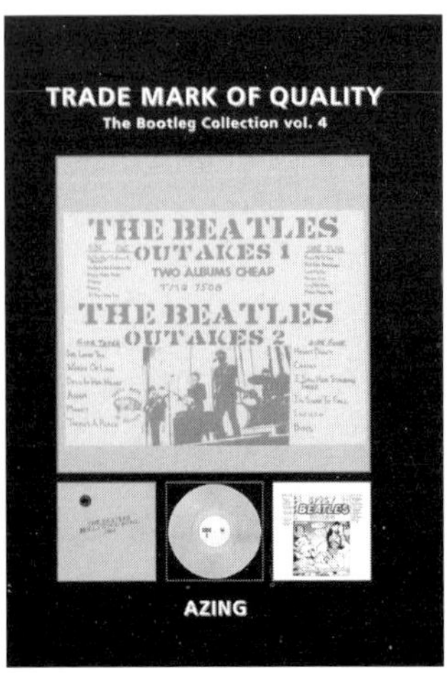
TRADE MARK OF QUALITY
The Bootleg Collection vol. 4
THE BEATLES
OUTTAKES 1
TWO ALBUMS CHEAP
THE BEATLES
OUTTAKES 2
AZING

AMAZING BEATLES
Het volledige platenverhaal - deel 1
BEATLES
AZING

AMAZING BEATLES
Het volledige platenverhaal - deel 2
AZING

PLEASE PLEASE ME
The Album Collection vol. 1
AZING

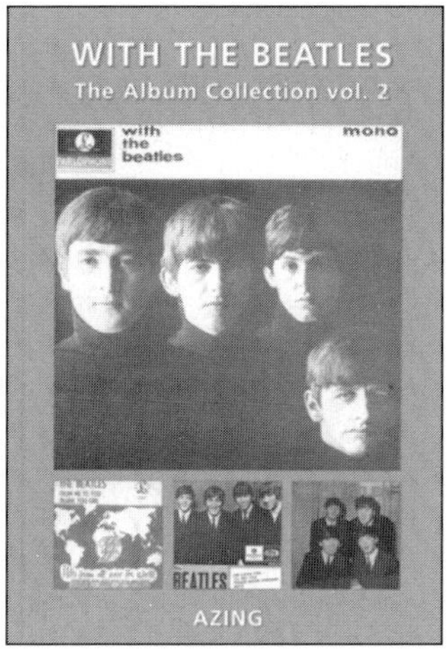
WITH THE BEATLES
The Album Collection vol. 2
AZING

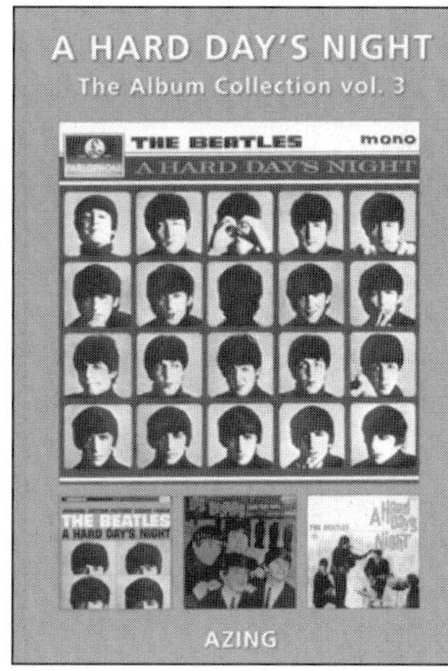
A HARD DAY'S NIGHT
The Album Collection vol. 3
AZING

BEATLES FOR SALE
The Album Collection vol. 4
AZING

HELP!
The Album Collection vol. 5
AZING

RUBBER SOUL
The Album Collection vol. 6
AZING

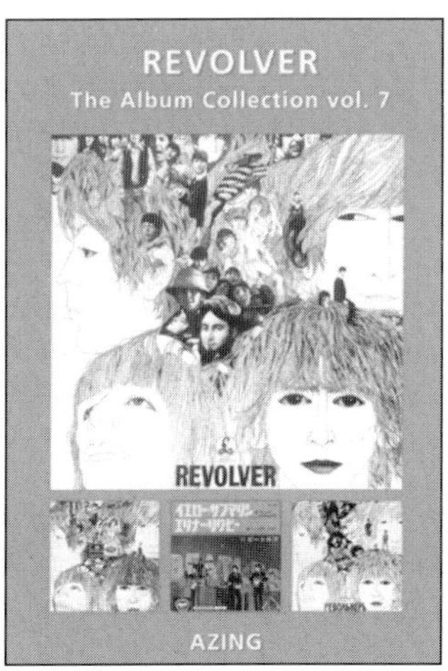
REVOLVER
The Album Collection vol. 7
AZING

SGT. PEPPER'S
LONELY HEARTS CLUB BAND
The Album Collection vol. 8
AZING

MAGICAL MYSTERY TOUR
The Album Collection vol. 9
AZING

Also available now!!!